JACK CURTIS

BLOOD TO BURN

POCKET BOOKS

New York   London   Toronto   Sydney   Tokyo   Singapore

An *Original* Publication of POCKET BOOKS

POCKET BOOKS, a division of Simon & Schuster Inc.
1230 Avenue of the Americas, New York, NY 10020

Copyright © 1992 by the Curtis Family Trust

ISBN: 0-671-74040-7

First Pocket Books printing September 1992

10 9 8 7 6 5 4 3 2 1

POCKET and colophon are registered trademarks of Simon & Schuster Inc.

Cover art by Lino Saffioti

Printed in the U.S.A.

A Stranger on the Open Kansas Road

Something was nagging at the back of Sam Benbow's mind, call it sixth sense, or instinct, or a primitive gut sense of danger. . . .

As he was about to give it up and blame his nervousness on the ham and eggs and flapjacks he had for breakfast, he saw the hack come to the bridge and start to cross, and then the driver yank the reins of the horse, bringing it to a sudden halt. The driver sat in the shadows for a moment, then proceeded on.

Sam prepared to come out of his covert, then he saw the stranger take off at a fast trot. . . .

Sam kicked his mount into a gallop after the hack, which was now going as fast as the livery nag could pull it. Despite the lashing whip of the burly driver, the old horse couldn't maintain the pace, so that in half a mile Sam came up alongside and yelled, "Whoa!" grabbing the head stall and bringing it to a stop.

"Hey! What you doin'?" the big man yelled and cocked the whip as if ready to lay it onto Sam himself.

"Don't do that, mister. Just tell me who you are and why you're trailin' me, and you can go on your way. I'd as liefer not have to beat it out of you," Sam said levelly, dismounting and approaching the brawny city dude. . . .

Books by Jack Curtis

Blood to Burn*
Paradise Valley*
The Jury on Smoky Hill*
Blood Cut*
Texas Rules*
The Sheriff Kill*
Red Knife Valley
Eagles Over Big Sur
Banjo
Klootchman

*Published by POCKET BOOKS

BLOOD TO BURN

Dusk brought a lavender blush over the western horizon along with the natural vespers of cicadas, prairie owls, and distant coyotes, accented by a grumpy dog's bark across town.

The small Kansas village named Sylvan Grove by a romantic land developer, who had also named Shady Bend and Arboreal Splendor downriver, closed its doors. A few coal oil lamps were lighted for the Bible readers, bread makers, and sock darners. Older men sat back in their rocking chairs for a last pipe of the day, while the children went to bed after saying their prayers.

Iridescent pigeons settled in the eaves of barns where stabled horses drowsed and brown family cows chewed their cuds as they rested in grassy back lots close to home. Main Street was dark except for the Red Rose Card Parlor, which also served as a saloon for the few town topers and occasional drummers bored to death from selling lace, ribbon, swiss, and rickrack.

Sometimes sitting at a poker table would be the prematurely aged man whose short-cut hair and mustache had turned white as goose down. Though he was hardly more than forty, the netted lines of pain and shock made an old man of him. Partly responsible for that mask of defeat was the gloved wooden hand attached to his left wrist. The fingers had been carved so that the hand looked half-closed, making it seem more natural, and he had developed such a skill with it that he could shuffle a deck of cards without worrying his fellow players.

For all of the signs of a disastrous life, this man, known as William Greer, managed to keep his features composed and serene, as if he had conquered the mistakes of the past, and his spirit had won over the miseries of the flesh.

His benign bearing, along with the premature aging, had earned him the sobriquet of "Uncle Billy."

He was not known to work for a living. How could he with only one hand? Quietly he parried any questions concerning the missing member, but it was generally thought he had lost it in the Civil War, and that he received a pension for his disability.

He had arrived in Sylvan Grove two years before, settling in so quietly that it seemed he'd been born there, especially after he rented Mrs. O'Banion's little house at the south edge of town where he could putter around with his chickens and garden, and invent things in his workshop, keeping to himself when he felt like it.

Once a month he rode over to Ellsworth on the black gelding he kept in Dad Aufdemburg's livery stable, and everyone assumed it was to pick up his pension money, because his wallet was considerably thicker with greenbacks when he returned, and he would loan a friend or neighbor a few dollars if the debt would be repaid within the month.

Children liked him because he often carried a bag of peppermints in his coat pocket, and spoke gently with them, ready to hear any sad tale of a stubbed toe or loose tooth.

It was also known that he'd helped the widow O'Banion make an emergency trip to Chicago when her father lay dying.

In these small ways, William Greer had made himself into a respected citizen of the small town, and though there was vicious gossip concerning his relationship with his neighbor and landlady, the widow Ruby O'Banion, there had never been any evidence of misconduct.

The one singular aspect of the man that no one could account for was the Remington .44 revolver he always wore on his hip, even though there hadn't been a major crime or even a threat of one in the short history of Sylvan Grove.

None of the other townsmen wore six-guns, and only the wild cowboys drifting through town had the same attachment to their weapons.

In time, even that rare feature became so commonplace that it was simply accepted as part of the man's life and so forgotten.

Only when William Greer didn't come back from his monthly ride to Ellsworth did the six-gun gain significance, and only after a cowboy out looking for strays discovered his body did his whole life come into question.

Not so much that he was dead did he become a mystery to Sylvan Grove, it was that his wooden hand had been burned off as well as the living stump of wrist. There were other marks of torture on his body, to such a degree that Doc Wade pronounced death due to heart failure brought on by the shock of so much pain.

Around the Red Rose, his friends murmured their guesses and projections, all agreeing that if Uncle Billy's torturers were trying to learn his secret, they had failed . . .

——————————————— **2** ———

Coming into Sullivan's Tavern and Oyster Emporium,
Sam Benbow stepped aside as an old swamper pushed
at the week's dirty sawdust with his broom, murmured a "Good morning, Johnny" to the old man,
and proceeded to the bar, where he ordered half a
dozen oysters on the half shell and a glass of beer for
his Monday morning breakfast from Tim Sullivan
himself.

Sam Benbow, a big man with bulldogger shoulders
and a plain face distinguished by a bent nose, a hard
lantern jaw, scarred cheekbones, and deep-seated
eyes, seemed out of place in the Oyster Emporium.
His rumpled frock coat, unpressed striped pants, and
dusty Wellington boots made him look like a maverick
cowpuncher fixing to go to his first funeral.

"Seen Skofer around?" Sam asked the portly Irishman, finishing up his beer.

"Can't you hear the old cuss?" Sullivan growled.

"I hear the wailin' of a banshee and a squallin' pig
with his tail in a crack."

"Take a look in the back room." Sullivan smiled.

Sam shook his head warily, and opened the door to the back room, where in the evening men played cards and politicians made deals.

Seated at a green-baize-covered poker table was a small rail of a man dressed in indigo pants and shirt, slowly waving his hands back and forth like an orchestra conductor and singing in a mournful voice:

> "Drink to me only with thine eyes
> And I will pledge with mine . . ."

His watery blue eyes were fixed on a large, long-haired shepherd named Rip, a street dog belonging to no one and everyone.

When Skofer hit a certain descending, grief-stricken pitch, Rip poked his nose toward the ceiling and cried out his own unknown grief.

"That's better, Rip," Skofer said, "let's go on with it so we got it right."

> "And leave a kiss in the cup
> And I'll not look for wine . . ."

Howling in harmony, the pair worked on their duet as Sam closed the door, cocked his head, shrugged his shoulders, and said to Sullivan, "Now he thinks he's a tenor."

"I think Rip has the better voice." Sullivan nodded.

"But he doesn't know the words." Sam let a little smile groove his thin cheeks, and went on out into the street.

We've got to get out of here, he reflected. This city life is too mushy for both of us. I'm getting old and fat, and Skofer's goin' crazy.

The South Texas Stockman's Association had thought he might help them with the Kansas legislators in creating a permanent cattle trail northward across the state, and had sent him to Topeka to represent their interests. But the legislators were more interested in bringing in more sodbusters, not more longhorns, and if they were listening to any particular special interests, it was the railroads who were in the saddle, and the railroads wanted the land settled and producing.

There was still big country left up around Wyoming and Montana, or west in New Mexico and Arizona territory, but Kansas was closing out the cowboys.

Maybe I should join the army, Sam thought. Once in a while, when the Indians came at you, it might be some exciting, a hell of a lot better than hanging around Topeka, Kansas, wasting time.

Climbing the stairway to his office above the drugstore, he asked himself for the thousandth time why didn't he settle down, find a decent job, get married, go to church, and grow old gracefully.

He felt a stiffness in his knees as he went up the stairs, and he thought his breath was a little short when he reached the top. Then he worried that he had so much time on his hands, he was worrying over nothing.

The office was just large enough to hold his rolltop desk and a couple of chairs. He'd left the walls unadorned except for a spare six-gun and its belt and holster hanging on a nail, and a hook for his flat-topped slouch hat.

Seated at the desk, he rummaged through the drawers, looking at old wanted posters, checking the calendar to make sure he wasn't forgetting some important business.

Even the damned cattle thieves were thinning out so fast that checking herd brands was becoming just a matter of routine.

Comes time for the rockin' chair, he thought, Sam Benbow won't have a front porch to put it on.

Hearing footsteps coming hesitantly up the stairway, he assumed it was Skofer trying to walk softly so as not to inflame his headache beyond repair, and he barked, "Get your butt in here, you old fool!"

There was no sound or reply.

Quickly striding to the door and jerking it open, ready to grab old Skofer by the front of his shirt, Sam was dumbfounded to see a young lady clutching at her handbag, staring up at him in terror.

"I beg your pardon, miss!" Sam took a deep breath and sighed, "I thought . . ."

"I was someone else," she said tentatively, seeing his embarrassment flushing up over his rocky face. "Odd," she added, "I thought only girls blushed."

"Sam Benbow at your service," he said heavily. "Please come in."

"Thank you. I've been trying to find you."

Dark-haired, with deep blue eyes, young, she wore a simple cotton dress, which he would have bet his last five dollars she had made herself. There was a scrubbed country look about her. Then he saw the work-hardened hands and the muscular forearms.

A farm girl, but a girl no longer. Milked a lot of cows. With no wedding band, that made her almost an old maid.

Something else about her. A tiredness in her face, a slight bowing of her shoulders, and features that somehow resembled someone he'd known a long time ago.

"Please have a seat." He pushed a straight-backed

chair forward, and took his own swivel chair at the desk.

"You are Mr. Sam Benbow?"

"That's me."

"You were in the war?"

"I served under Jeb Stuart."

"And you were a cavalry captain?"

"How did you know that?"

"I didn't until just now."

"Who are you then?" he asked, trying to turn the questioning around.

"My name is Elizabeth Faraday. I've lived most of my life on a dairy farm near Veitengruber, Missouri, and I'm here because of a letter."

Opening her knitted handbag, she removed a folded sheet of tablet paper and handed it to Sam.

"Been around awhile . . ." he commented, unfolding the page and reading.

> Dear Elizabeth Faraday, Bill Greer asked me to send this to you in case something bad happened to him, and I'm doing it. He was a good man and deserved better treatment.
> Mrs. Henry (Ruby) O'Banion.

"And what did she send you?" Sam asked.

"First let me explain, I don't know anyone named Bill Greer," Elizabeth said, bringing out a piece of stiff white cardboard with a new twenty-dollar gold piece glued on it. Beneath it, in a steady hand, was written:

> Dear Bess, I guess if you read this it means I'm a goner. You go find Captain Sam Benbow. Tell him I'd like him to look into this matter. Last I heard he worked for the Stockman's Association

in San Antonio. Tell him I'd like him to make it right. Remember, this coin is not the first nor the last when the chickens come home to roost.
Your Dad,
Bill Faraday.

"Do you know where this came from?" Sam asked.

"There wasn't anything on the envelope." She shook her head and looked at the floor.

"Seems like he could have told us something more," Sam said, wondering what she was holding back.

"I think he wanted to say as little as possible because of my family," she said uncertainly.

"I recall he was newly married when the war broke out."

"To my mother," Elizabeth nodded, "but he'd come up from the South, not knowing there'd be a war. He met her in Saint Louis, fell in love, and followed her home."

"He was a romantic youngster." Sam nodded. "Always wore a long, curly feather in his hatband."

"I think he meant to take Ma back to his folks' place in Georgia, but when the war started, she didn't want to go, and he had to fight for the South."

And, Sam thought as he remembered the dashing young cavalier, by the time the war was over, there wasn't any homeplace to go back to. Sherman and his bummers had taken care of that.

"He was wounded at Chickamauga. We took a beating there." Sam unconsciously probed the dimple in his right leg with his fingers as the memory of that day came back. "His horse was killed and he ended up in a crater full of dying soldiers. Lost his hand there and his hair turned white. Bad day for us."

"I remember him when he came back," Elizabeth said. "I was about six. He rode into the farm on a black horse. I was fascinated by his wooden hand. No one recognized him, not even Ma. He looked so old."

Sam compressed his lips as he thought of how many blows the happy-go-lucky youth had taken in such a few short years.

More than that, after Sam had been shot off his horse when they came up against Joseph Hooker's troops at Gettysburg, young Billy Faraday had ridden across the open field of fire, leaned down from the saddle, and caught Sam's left hand, then dragged him off into a ravine where the Confederates had set up a first aid station.

Later on, down in Tennessee, when Sam had learned Billy was hurt in the crater full of dead and dying, Sam had gone out and returned the favor.

He hadn't seen him since that day, because Billy had been sent back to Georgia while Sam stayed on until the bitter, bitter end.

"War is truly hell," Sam said heavily, "but I must say, it brings out the best in the men who live through it."

"You knew him well then?" she asked softly, touched by the heaviness of his mood.

"I owe him my life," Sam said simply. "I guess we better go find him, or what's left of him."

"But where?"

"I need that envelope, Miss Faraday," Sam said stiffly.

"I don't have it." Her cheeks flushed red and her eyes went down to the floor again.

"You've got to trust me. You can't do it alone."

"Don't tell me what I can't do!" she retorted sharply.

"Then I'm going over to Veitengruber."

"I can't go back there," she said, clenching her strong hands together nervously. "Never."

"I might need some help," he said, wondering what was going on behind those determined blue eyes.

"You'll find the whole tribe on their farms just west of Veitengruber, and you won't need any help from me."

"May I keep this awhile?" Sam asked, peeling the gold piece off the cardboard.

"I guess so." She rose and started for the door.

"Have you any money?"

"Enough to last till I find a job."

"What can you do?"

Turning back and setting her jaw stubbornly, she said, "I can do anything. You tell them that."

Elizabeth Faraday was amazed at herself as she left Sam Benbow's office. Raised on the farm under the strictest discipline, she'd been taught that women were made to serve men, that they were put on earth to work at the lowest, dirtiest jobs, and that they should not speak in the presence of their betters.

She'd been permitted to go to the school in the village of Veitengruber, but only after she'd done half a day's work beforehand, and afterward too, and it had been a miracle she'd learned to read and write and cipher numbers, a miracle she'd created by snatching precious minutes away from the cornfield, and the corn sheller, from the milking in the cowbarn, and the mucking out later on, from the churn and from the cheese press, from the hoe and the rake, from the soapmaking to the scrubboard.

For that reason, she was amazed that she could talk forthrightly with Sam Benbow. Of course, she thought, he was an easy man to talk to. She'd been unprepared for that. She'd thought he'd be a crusty old war veteran, or a cigar-smoking sot bent on stealing her goods, but he'd turned out to be just a rumpled-up cattleman, uncomfortable in his city clothes. Maybe he was a little afraid of her, even though he'd talked hard and direct, almost hostile when she'd lied.

She wished now she'd brought the envelope along, but she had been afraid to trust someone she didn't know, even if her dad had recommended him. She'd thought it better to hold it back, wait and see, make sure Sam Benbow qualified before committing everything.

Thinking about it, she felt a strange thrill at meeting the big, shaggy man and speaking up and holding her own.

They would have whipped her with the buggy whip for being so brave over on the farm.

How they liked to sit in judgment, the old man and his sons, and say, "She was out walking in the grass barefoot instead of hoeing her row. For that, Olaf, give her five lashes with the buggy whip."

And they were all the harder on her because her mother had gotten married without their permission, and then, because her mother didn't have her man to defend her, they'd beaten her down so that in a few years she would submit to anything they demanded, growing into a vague shape in a long cotton dress and sunbonnet, working from dawn and through the day and on into the night. Every day except Sunday, when all that the women had to do was feed and milk the cows, feed the chickens, gather the eggs, swill the pigs, get dressed for church, then return to cook the Sunday dinner, wash the dishes, then milk the cows again, skim the cream off the morning's milk, find wood for the fire, mend and darn, and so to bed.

Her mother hardly spoke anymore; her knees were

bowed and hurting from pitching hay and shucking corn. She acted as if she wanted to die and go to heaven.

Witnessing the ruin of her mother had given impetus to Elizabeth's desire for independence.

She'd run away once when she was fifteen. Just run. Didn't know where she was going, but after an undeserved whipping, she'd decided anything was better than such a homelife.

They'd caught her before she'd gone five miles, and they had whipped her, tied her to the bed overnight, and then whipped her again.

After that, she'd been too afraid to stray, let alone run off. All she'd been able to do with her life was to avoid an early marriage by being mean and obstinate with all the suitors her elders had picked for her until they'd said she wouldn't ever prove out as a wife and had left her alone.

For her contrariness, they'd laid all the more labor on her and all the more indignities on her, doing their best to break her spirit.

Only the image of her father on his black horse, his back straight, his haggard hawk's eyes still fighting against fate, his refusal to become a part of the Veitengruber scheme of forfeiture of life for more land and more corn and more cows to make more milk, only that remembrance of his unbending dignity had sustained her all these years.

Then the young stranger peddling tinware had come by the farm and asked to stay and work for his keep.

Rene. Rene Armenescu. A slim, handsome young man with soft brown eyes and black hair tumbling down over his ears in ringlets. He'd told her he wanted to study to become a lawyer.

His eyes seemed to say: *Trust me. Want me. I need you.*

The Veitengrubers had worked him, and hazed him, and forbidden him to speak to her.

He'd managed to give her an address in Topeka where she could find him if she could ever get up enough gumption to leave, and then he himself left after the men had held him down and singed his beautiful hair.

A few days later, she met the mailman on the road before he'd reached the farm, and he'd given her the letter that she knew would set her free if she would be courageous and strong as her father had wanted her to be.

Now she knew two men in Topeka, Sam Benbow and Rene Armenescu, and all she needed was a room of her own and a job.

Comparing Sam Benbow with Rene Armenescu, she couldn't help but wonder why Sam had been so rigid and forbidding when he talked to her, and how pleasant and hopeful Rene was with her. Rene would make a good lawyer, she thought. He spoke so well and was so elegant in his manners, whereas Sam Benbow, after all, was just a veteran of a lot of battles that had finally left him stranded. No past, no future.

He was like the Veitengrubers in a way. He wouldn't change his ways to fit the times, whereas Rene was always looking to the future, thinking up ways to help her achieve independence.

Unconsciously she compared the two men, and as she saw the sign Waitress Wanted in the window of Ira's Lunch, she thought, Rene will want me to find a better job, but Sam Benbow wouldn't care one way or the other.

While Elizabeth Faraday was asking for a job, Sam was studying the gold coin carefully and thinking about Billy Faraday, the bright, laughing boy who rode like a fury in battle, and wept whenever a comrade fell.

The coin appeared to be newly minted. The O below the date indicated it had been minted in New Orleans. The stamped portrait of Liberty facing left, surrounded by thirteen stars, made no impression on him. He'd need to ask someone who knew coins.

It hadn't been marked up or hollowed out, or even used. It was simply an extremely shiny uncirculated gold piece dated 1879, some three years old.

Why wouldn't Elizabeth Faraday want to return home? Was she holding back the envelope with a return address or postmark?

Beneath all that scoured-clean milkmaid appearance, what was she really like?

"Where the heck is Skofer?"

He might remember something.

They'd all rode with Jeb Stuart, but it had affected Skofer differently than it had Sam or Billy. Skofer had been a professor at the University of Virginia, and the war had ruined his faith in the goodness of humanity. He'd never wanted to return to the academic life.

Sam slipped the coin into his vest pocket, put on his slouch hat, and went down the stairs to Topeka Avenue, turned left and strolled half a block to the First Charter Bank of Kansas, and entered the hushed, high-ceilinged room.

After withdrawing enough money from his account to make the trip over to Missouri and seeing that his balance was a hundred dollars from zero, he nodded to Elijah Sark, the head banker himself, whose desk was separated from the rest of the room by a walnut railing.

"How's business, Mr. Sark?"

"Couldn't be better." Sark beamed, his porky head nodding mechanically.

"I wonder if you could tell me if this coin means anything special?" Sam fished out the gold piece and handed it over to the banker.

After a brief hesitation, the banker frowned as if he'd just sucked a pickle, and asked, "Where'd you get it?"

"Is it counterfeit?" Sam asked, bothered by the sudden change in the banker's humor.

"No. It's just a twenty-dollar gold piece." The banker handed back the coin. "There's nothing unusual about it, except it looks new."

"Probably been in a bank vault."

"Maybe." Sark nodded. "Where'd you say it come from?"

"I won it from a stranger in a poker game," Sam lied.

"I don't believe in gambling." Sark's eyes fixed on Sam's as if they could somehow wring the truth out of him.

"And you've got the bank to prove it." Sam smiled.

Riding the Santa Fe that night over to Saint Joe, Sam had plenty of time to try to put little Billy Faraday back together again.

Little Billy . . . always joking, always ready to give something extra to cheer up the men, always tinkering with gadgets. How had he ever gotten a wife in Missouri?

Yet it wasn't so unusual. A great many Missourians had come from the South to settle the state before the war. Perhaps the Veitengrubers were originally from Georgia or the Carolinas. Maybe they were large landowners.

Little Billy . . . maybe eighteen years old, fresh from the Georgia academy, spending the summer traveling, broadening his knowledge, likely thinking of going on to California for the winter before returning home to help out on the plantation.

No doubt his folks were some put out at his sudden plunge into matrimony, but they'd probably forgive and forget. The big hitch in Billy's plans was the damn war. He hadn't figured on that, but he was caught in the nutcracker. He had to go home and join up. Had to. No matter what his bride said, he couldn't ever go back on his family or the Confederacy.

Arriving early in the morning in Saint Joe, Sam took his time with a big breakfast, then hired a horse for the twelve-mile ride down to Veitengruber.

The countryside was settled and fenced, planted mostly to corn or timothy pasture.

The great two-and-a-half-story barns and the little, boxy houses nearby made an odd combination.

The grazing cattle were a mixture of Holstein, Jersey, Guernsey, and Shorthorn, nothing like the angular Texas longhorn that Sam was used to.

Sam thought nature was being crowded out by the farmer's passion for rectangles and triangles.

Down in Texas you put your house close to the water, build a few corrals for the range cattle and horses, and the rest is wide-open mesquite, cholla cactus, cocklebur, and devil's-claw. Your neighbor would be over at the next watering hole, maybe five miles or so.

Here the lane was bounded on both sides by rail fences, and occasional travelers rode in wagons or hacks.

The country wasn't ravaged like the South. There were no burned plantation houses with only chimneys left standing. There were no fields abandoned and going back under vines and saplings.

These people were prosperous!

Maybe Billy was smarter than he thought, Sam reflected. Of course, Billy might have had a problem adjusting to a farm instead of a cotton plantation, but if he could make a good living, then why not give it a try?

Riding the rented gelding through the peaceful countryside, touching his flat-topped hat occasionally as he passed a buggy or wagon, Sam didn't notice that a one-horse hack was following along the same road at the same speed as his own. Keeping a half mile behind, the hack's driver, a burly ex-pug wearing a checkered suit, derby hat, and street shoes, kept the space between them constant.

Big and beefy, with a flattened nose and close-set eyes, the man looked as if he should be on a tough street in Saint Louis rather than in the flat farming country of western Missouri.

Something was nagging at the back of Sam's mind, call it sixth sense, or instinct, or a primitive gut sense of danger.

He'd survived by trusting that nagging sense which was always so vague he felt foolish, but deep down he trusted it, and coming to a small, unfenced bridge that crossed a running creek, he pulled off and sent the horse downstream into a stand of cottonwoods.

Holding there, he watched the road for the phantom that was itching the back of his neck.

As he was about to give it up and blame his nervousness on the ham and eggs and flapjacks he'd had for breakfast, he saw the hack come to the bridge and start to cross, and then the driver yank the reins of the horse, bringing it to a sudden halt.

The driver sat in the shadows of the black, oiled canvas sides for a moment, then proceeded on.

Again Sam prepared to come out of his covert, when he saw the hack returning at a fast trot.

Stopping at the bridge, this time the driver climbed out to the ground and studied the side of the road.

Seeing Sam's tracks and glancing at the grove of cottonwoods, the big man knew he'd been caught and was furiously thinking of how best to handle his assignment.

He walked around the hack, as if waiting for someone, pulled out his watch from his vest pocket, checked it twice, then got back in the hack and sent the horse back toward Saint Joe.

Sam was puzzled. No one, not even Skofer, knew where he was going, except for Elizabeth Faraday. If she had set this mean-looking dude on his trail, why?

Only one way to find out.

Heading his mount back to the roadway, Sam kicked him into a gallop after the hack, which was going as fast as the livery nag could pull it.

Despite the lashing whip of the burly driver, the old horse couldn't maintain the pace, so that in half a mile Sam came up alongside, yelled, "Whoa!" and grabbed its headstall, bringing it to a stop.

"Hey! What you doin'?" the big man yelled, and cocked the whip as if ready to lay it onto Sam himself.

"Don't do that, mister," Sam said levelly. "Just tell me who you are and why you're trailin' me, and you can go on your way."

"I'll tell you nothin', mister," the big man said. "Leave go my horse."

"I'd as liefer not have to beat it out of you," Sam said, dismounting, and approaching the brawny city dude.

"I'm a businessman," the dude said. "I'm lookin' for some property to buy."

"Listen to me, dude," Sam said softly. "I remember you gettin' on the train at Topeka. We are going to

20

have a regular Irish jig if you don't change your tune. Now, who the hell are you?"

"Leave me be!" the big man blustered, and swung the whip at Sam's face.

Sam dodged to one side as the popper stung him on the cheek.

The next time the whip lashed out, he moved in under it, caught the braided leather, and yanked the whip free. Throwing it aside, he grabbed the big man by the arm and jerked him out of the hack.

Sam realized too late that it was too easy.

The dude came down on Sam with such force, Sam went over backward and felt the man's knees slam into his chest, driving the wind out of him.

Before he could get his breath, the beefy dude kicked him in the ribs and was set to kick him again when Sam seized his ankle and jerked him off balance. Still gripping the ankle as the big man went down, he gave it a hard twist that brought a scream of pain from the heavier man.

Climbing to his feet, Sam waited for the dude to collect himself, hoping he'd seen the light and was ready to discuss the problem.

"You ready?" Sam asked.

The stranger got to his knees, but instead of coming on up to his feet, lunged forward, tackled Sam, driving him back to the ground again, and with a trained, professional rhythm, commenced swinging short right and left chops before Sam could get his hands up.

Sam rolled aside and came around with a hard right hand that popped against the skull of the big dude and slowed him down some, and then followed with a left hook that took the big man on the jaw, loosening his teeth. The dude rolled away and got to his feet at the same time as Sam came driving at him with a powerful overhand right that landed just below his ear and sent him reeling.

"You all stop this right now!" a voice said, and Sam turned a moment to see three mounted men dressed in overalls and hickory shirts looking down at him from their big mules.

The middle man had a double-barreled goose gun aimed at Sam's middle.

"What's this ruckus all about?" one of the farmers asked sternly.

"He's followin' me," Sam croaked, fighting to get his breath back.

"He's lyin'!" the big man said. "He tried to hold me up."

"Who are you? Where you from?" The other farmer addressed Sam.

"I'm Sam Benbow from Topeka, Kansas, and I'm tellin' you the truth."

"You talk like a southerner," the farmer with the goose gun said.

"Ask him who *he* is!" Sam blazed back.

"All right, stranger, who be you and where from?"

"My name is George Brown and I'm from Kansas City, Missouri."

"Why are you followin' me?" Sam demanded.

"I'm not. I'm on business of my own, and you ought to be hung for robbin' innocent folks on the roads."

"What do you reckon, Olaf?" the old man asked the one with the shotgun.

"Where you goin', Mr. Benbow?" Olaf asked.

"I'm looking for the Veitengruber family."

"You're close," the old man said. "Now, where you goin', Mr. Brown?"

"I'm goin' to Saint Joe," the burly dude said.

"Then both you git where you're goin'," the old

man said. "We don't allow fightin' in the roads of De Kalb County."

In frustration Sam mounted his horse as the dude climbed into the hack.

"I hope to see you again, Brown, or whatever you call yourself," Sam said.

"Likely you will, and likely I'll break your neckbones next time," the big man yelled back, and slapped the reins on his horse's rump.

Before Sam could leave, the old farmer frowned meanly. "Happens we are Veitengrubers, me'n Olaf, and Herman. We are goin' along with you and see what you got to say for yourself."

"Fine with me," Sam said. "That man was lying."

"The world is full of liars," Olaf said.

"And few left to praise the Lord," Herman said piously, raising his eyes heavenward.

They rode along without speaking for a couple of miles, then took a side road off northerly.

"The town is just over that rise, but were goin' home," the old man said, and led the way up a rutted track.

Passing by neat and tidy cornfields where men in overalls as well as women wearing sunbonnets were hoeing weeds between the plants, Sam thought, this is the way the whole Big Pasture will be in another ten years.

"Lots of work," he said.

"Keeps folks out of mischief." The old man nodded.

An occasional cultivator pulled by a single mule tilled the soil between the rows.

"That must get kind of tiresome, lookin' at the mule's butt all day," Sam tried again.

"It makes the increase," the old man said. "The

more we work, the more we make, the more we save, the more land we can buy. Work makes increase."

"Interestin'," Sam said, thinking it sounded dull as hell.

Coming into a lane that led between fenced-in dairy cattle, they arrived at what Sam figured was the original homeplace.

The barn was smaller and cruder than the others; the house was built of stone and logs.

"You build this yourself?" Sam asked the old man.

"I did."

"You know a man named Bill Faraday?"

The old man glared at him and said, "Come inside."

He led the way through the back door into a large kitchen which served as the dining room as well. A plank table with benches occupied the middle of the room, and the old man said, "Set."

Women wearing large sunbonnets concealing their faces moved back and forth from the stove to the water bucket, to the storage bins, not speaking, gray ghosts, faceless, shapeless.

To the side, one of these gray shapes was ironing shirts with a heavy, sad iron, one of several that she had heating on the big range.

The kitchen smelled of bread dough, pork stew, and boiled sauerkraut. There was no aroma of coffee.

Sam took a seat at the table and decided to wait them out. "Buttermilk?" the old man asked in a crackling voice.

"No, thanks."

"Why do you want to see that fool Faraday?" the old man asked, taking the seat across from Sam while his sons sat on either side of him.

"Why are you so contrary when his name comes up?"

"He nearly destroyed my plan."

"Have you seen him lately?"

"Who are you?"

"I'm a stock inspector, looking for an old army friend."

"Better he should have died in the war," the old man said.

"I'm inclined to agree with you right now," Sam said. "The crazy kid I knew could never fit in here."

"He could have fit in if he had worked."

"Couldn't work with just one hand." The chinless one called Olaf grinned. "We used to hide his wooden hand when he'd take it off to wash."

"We give him and Naomi the attic until he could take up the next claim and build his own house. We fed him," the old man added.

"But he didn't make any increase."

"How could he with only one hand? He couldn't shovel manure, he couldn't hoe, he couldn't even milk. He just wanted to tinker with inventions that never worked."

"I knew him as a fighter," Sam said quietly.

"A fighter for slavery?"

"I hope it was for something more than that, like keeping the government close to home, where it belongs."

"You was a slaveholder?"

"No, sir," Sam said. "My folks raised cattle. We never owned another man or woman, nor tried to tell other folks how to run their business."

"I want to know why you're looking for Faraday."

"Because I think he's become very rich," Sam said, hoping the old man's greed would pop something loose.

"He couldn't." The old man shook his head. "He was a worthless fool."

"What happened to his wife? She might be in line for a large fortune."

"We declared Faraday dead after one year, and she married a cousin," the old man said.

The shapeless, faceless lady dropped the sad iron to the plank floor, then, putting a burned knuckle to her mouth, turned and hurried outside while the other ladies moved about as if nothing had happened.

No wonder Billy left, Sam thought. He wasn't interested so much in increase as he was in happiness.

"He came back here to start a new life," Sam said.

"Why didn't he just stay with his other life?" Herman growled meanly. "And leave us alone."

"His other life was destroyed. The plantation burned and abandoned, his people all dead or maimed. There wasn't anyting left."

"Where did he get the fortune you're talkin' about?" The old man stuck to the point.

"I don't know yet. I've got to find out where he went from here."

"There were letters from Louisiana, but I burned them," the old man said.

"What part of Louisiana?"

"I don't recall. He finally give up writin'. I thank God for that."

"Why?"

"We'd had a hard enough time gettin' him to leave, and I sure didn't want him to come back."

"Who were the letters addressed to?"

"My granddaughter, Elizabeth."

"She didn't get to read them?"

"My people read what I tell them to," the old man said. "If there's something my granddaughter shouldn't read, she don't get to read it."

"You folks ever been out of De Kalb County?" Sam asked, feeling tired and sick.

26

"We goin' to own De Kalb County in another twenty years." Tall Herman smiled. "Maybe change the name to Veitengruber County, Missouri. How'd that suit you, stranger?"

"It'd suit me just fine. Every time I give my horse a bait of corn, I'll remember you." Sam got up from the bench.

"Just a minute," the old man said. "Naomi bore that man a child, and she should inherit his fortune."

"But you declared him dead years ago," Sam said, "and he didn't even have rags enough to pad a crutch then."

"You're jokin' me now." The old man rose sternly, his bristly gray hair rising like a rooster's hackles. "We don't fun about money."

"There's no money unless I can find it," Sam said, "and I can't find it unless I know where he went from here."

"I figure you know more'n that," the old man said. "You ain't leavin' till you tell it."

"You're wrong, old man," Sam said plainly. "I'm not any of yours, and I don't want to be."

"There's somethin' else, ain't there? It's Elizabeth. That's how you got onto us. She got the mail one day and started actin' fidgety. She been to see you?"

"Elizabeth?" Sam countered.

"She's half-Veitengruber, but she's got the same problem Naomi had before we beat some sense into her."

"What has any of this got to do with Billy Faraday?" Sam asked, backing off toward the door.

"Elizabeth is my grandchild, but the blood is bad," the old man said with a touch of melancholy. "She grew up learnin' how to work, but then she became a wanton. Any but her would have give me that mail and not lied about it."

"I suppose you wanted her to marry a cousin, and she had different ideas," Sam said.

"She took up with a gypsy. We singed his hair and punished him some, and then threw him out."

"He mighta been part Indian or something," Herman said. "For sure he didn't know nothin' about workin' corn."

"Called hisself Rene Armenescu!" Olaf hooted. "Can you imagine anybody with a name like that!"

"Did Elizabeth get mail regularly, or just that one time?" Sam asked.

"How would I know?" the old man answered. "She was a liar and a wanton, and when we dog her down, I'll whip her until she learns her place."

"I just doubt if she'll be back."

"We'll fetch her back. Then we'll punish her. We are all one family, working together for the increase."

"Besides, there ain't no way for a woman to make a livin' on her own," tall Herman declared.

"I've known some that did pretty well, and had a good time doin' it, too."

"She wouldn't do such a thing," chinless Olaf said.

"I can't think of any reason why not." Sam headed for the door.

"Just a minute—" Olaf lifted the goose gun.

The gray-cowled women seemed to disappear in the gloom, leaving Sam and the three Veitengrubers to their manly business.

Sam slowly turned and said quietly, "Ever shoot a man?"

"I guess there's always a first time," the chinless farmer grinned. "You don't go until Pa tells you."

"My friend," Sam said, "I suppose I've killed somewhere around a hundred and fifty by now, and it's never been a pleasure to me. Now, put down that goose gun before you become a part of the decrease."

"You don't scare me none," Olaf said.

"What I'm goin' to do is not kill you," Sam said, holding his gaze concentrated on Olaf's face. "I'm goin' to blow your knee to pieces, and then I'll always wonder how long the Veitengrubers will carry a cripple before puttin' the run on him."

"You ain't even got a gun!" Olaf smiled.

"That's your second mistake."

"Don't shoot him in the kitchen," the old man said. "That buckshot makes an unholy mess."

"Outside, mister," Olaf said, waggling the long two-bore at Sam.

"Which door?" Sam asked, and as the old man stepped forward to open the back door, Sam grabbed him around the neck with his left hand, and drew the .36 navy Colt from under his frock coat.

Keeping the old man between himself and the shotgun, Sam held the Colt against the old man's bristly head, and said, "All right, Olaf, you just set that greener over in the corner and then back off."

The farmer in patched overalls turned a sickly pale and asked, "Pa?"

"Do it."

Lowering the hammers carefully, Olaf set the goose gun up against the wall and backed off toward his tall brother, whose mouth was hanging open like a loose flap.

"Now, I'm goin' out of here in one piece, or this old man's goin' to be kickin' around out in the yard like a chopped rooster, understand?"

"Yes, sir," Herman said.

Sam dragged the old man out through the door, and as he shoved him away to mount the big bay, Olaf came to the door, the goose gun arcing down to cut Sam in two. Sam fired quickly, instinctively, as if he'd already been through the scene many times before and this was just another rehearsal.

His seventy-grain bullet passed through the patched right knee of the overall and struck the knee with almost a hundred foot-pounds of energy, cracking through the kneecap and shattering both sides of the knee as it passed on through.

The force of that single shot flipped the farmer into a backward pirouette that left him on the ground in less than half a second. The sharp report of the small Colt was lost in the thunder of the twelve-gauge firing harmlessly into the sky, and in that moment of stunned silence, Sam mounted the bay and held him at a slow trot back toward Kansas.

3

The burly ex-pug in the checkered suit was the first one off the afternoon train. He immediately hurried up Topeka Avenue.

Amidst faint cries of protest, the big man shouldered his way straight ahead like a hungry draft horse heading for the barn.

The door to the bank was locked, and a card in the window said HOURS 9–3.

He rattled and banged on the door with increasing ferocity until the banker, Elijah Sark himself, opened the door, peered about suspiciously, then whispered, "Get on in here, Basham, and don't make so damned much racket."

The interior of the long, high-ceilinged room was hushed and redolent of pine oil and musty money. A regulator clock solemnly ticktocked the hours away, with its brass pendulum measuring out the seconds.

"Come into the back room," Sark said, glaring up at the big bruiser.

They passed by the walnut counter with its turned

spool fence that separated the customers from the tellers and their money, and entered the back room, which contained a desk, chairs, and a black horsehide settee.

The man seated in the corner didn't get up nor offer to shake hands. Taller than Basham, but not so heavily muscled, there was an air of judgment on Weed's hatchet face, as if he were sizing up whatever he saw as to how fast he could kill it or destroy it. With those cold, merciless eyes, he sized up Basham and thought he could have him bleeding out on the floor in less than two seconds.

"Why are you back so early?" Sark demanded as soon as the door closed.

"You told me he was old and fat, gone to seed!" Basham protested. "I was following along way back, but he cut off and checked his back trail."

"So he's tricky," Weed grunted. "What'd you learn?"

"I learned he's got a hell of an overhand right." Basham touched the swollen side of his scarred and lumpy face.

"So he whipped you?" Weed glowered at him with his gray, icy stare.

"The hell he did. I had him down, but three damned farmers came along and took him away from me."

"Three farmers?" the banker asked doubtfully.

"One of them had a double-barrel shotgun pointed right at my guts," Basham said defensively. "Wasn't anything left to do but get back here."

"What happened to Benbow?" Weed asked, disgusted.

"They put him under the gun and marched him on down the road. I'm tellin' you, there was nothin' I could do about it."

"So you come runnin' back like a yeller dog!" Weed growled.

"Now, listen here, mister, nobody calls Bull Basham yellow!"

"Sit down before you make me puke," Weed said.

"I'm just sayin' I beat him up good, but nobody can go up against a twelve-gauge."

"Who were the farmers?" Sark asked intently.

"Just three clodhoppers in overalls," Bull said. "It was outside the town of Veitengruber."

"He'll be back if they don't kill him," Weed said thoughtfully. "But why was he goin' to Missouri?"

"It's just farms. Mostly Germans. You know, pig's feet and pickled beans." Basham sat down heavily. "If you'd tell me somethin' of what this is all about, maybe I could get the information faster."

"You don't need to know any more than you do already," Sark retorted, trying to think the situation through clearly.

"Then don't expect me to pass any miracles."

"Shut up," the banker said. "Chances are Benbow will be back on the morning train. We need to be ready with a plan."

"You're always makin' plans," Weed said, "and half the time they don't work."

"I've got the bank," Sark said defensively, "and that's just the beginning if—"

"The damned bank is nothin' more'n a piece of paper sayin' you owe more than you've got," Weed continued grimly. "How soon before you've got to run?"

"Nonsense, Weed!" Sark forced a smile. "We're making money, honest money."

"I know you too well, Sark," Weed growled. "I think I'll hang around the depot tomorrow and kill the son of a bitch when he gets off the train."

"No, no!" Sark protested. "We can use him!"

"Not after mush brain tipped him off that we're on to somethin'."

"I didn't tip off nothin'," Bull declared.

"Get out of here," Weed growled, his eyes probing through the layers of fat and muscle, right into Bull's secret and quaking heart.

"Fine with me." Bull went to the back door and turned to face Weed. "But don't call me yellow. I ain't afraid of you."

"I think you'd be fun to shoot in the belly." Weed let a jagged smile cross over his hatchet face.

"Just tell me. Where you from?" Bull tried to look like a daredevil.

"Ever hear of Ellsworth?" Weed sneered.

The name registered slowly as Basham's scrambled brain tried to match up Weed with Ellsworth. Finally the light dawned on his battered features.

"I got you now," he said. "You're the one they call Loco."

"That's me. Loco Weed. I been thinkin' I can kill you in less than a second. Break my record."

"Good-bye," Bull said, hustling out the back door.

"Damned fool," Weed sneered. "You're wastin' your money on him."

"He's the best I could find in a hurry," Elijah Sark said. "I wired you and hired him within an hour after Benbow brought in that gold piece."

"No mistakin' it for another stamping?"

"No. The date, the mint, the prooflike finish; it's one of ours."

"So all we have to do is find out where he got it," Weed said. "I can burn him some and he'll talk."

"You tried that, and look what it got us!" the jowly banker protested. "This time we let Benbow lead us to the goods."

34

"The other one could stand some pain. I don't think your Benbow can, if you're right about him bein' gone to seed. Those old gunfighters, they begin to like livin' after so long a time."

"No, Weed, this time we go slow. You can kill him when we've got our money back."

"I'll burn him and bleed him," Weed sneered, thinking that when the time came, there'd be two cozy corpses instead of one lying side by side.

Returning on the morning train from Saint Joe, Sam was bone-weary from the rattling of the train, the smoke and cinders coming through the open windows, the gabble of a Danish group all set to colonize Kansas and make a new little Denmark, and his neck was stiff from trying to sleep sitting up.

He had spent his time and money on almost nothing, and he had neither resource to waste, he thought as the train came to a stop.

The man in the checkered suit had been his one chance to solve the riddle of Billy Faraday, but the nosy Veitengrubers had to get in the way, and he felt no pleasure from crippling the farmer.

A sensible gunman facing a shotgun at close range would have shot him through the heart, he reflected, stepping from the coach to the rough plank decking of the depot platform.

But then if I'd killed him, they'd have had a posse on me all the way to Saint Joe. Could have taken him in the shoulder with the same effect, except I told him what I'd do. What's the difference between a stiff shoulder and a stiff knee when you're lookin' at the hind end of a mule all day?

Hell with 'em. Where was Billy?

Went to Louisiana.

Louisiana was like a big country thousands of miles

away. You might as well be in heaven as Louisiana, Billy, Sam thought.

Never forget that looped-up kossuth hat with the big, curly white feather sweeping around and the gray cape with the bright brass buttons and gold braid. What a dandy you were!

Sam made his way to the main street and stopped at Sullivan's for a glass of beer to clear the cinders from his throat.

"Seen Skofer lately?" Sam asked the red-faced Irishman, making himself a cheese and ham sandwich from the free lunch.

"He's around somewhere. Been moanin' that you abandoned him to the enemy."

"Next thing I know, he'll be teaching Mrs. Hogg's pigs to yodel," Sam smiled.

"Been travelin'?"

"Some. Learned never to give a farmer credit for the brains of a pissant."

"But they keep comin'," Sullivan said. "I'm thinkin' of movin' on towards Dodge City."

"I'm thinking more on Powder River," Sam said.

"You know the difference between a sheepherder in Scotland and a sheepherder in Texas?"

"Tell me." Sam smiled.

"In Scotland when a feller sees a sheepman comin' down the road with his critters, he says, 'Behold the gentle shepherd with his fleecy flock!' Now, in Texas, that same feller says when he sees the same feller comin' over the ridge with the same sheep, he says, 'Look at the crazy son of a bitch with his goddamn woollies!'"

Sam laughed, cocked his hat back, tossed a dime on the counter, and said, "If you see Skofer, tell him I need him."

I've got to get out of this town, he told himself,

walking up the street and entering the new brick federal building. On the second floor was the Department of Justice, which meant the headquarters of the two eastern Kansas federal marshals.

Of the two, one was gone and the other was on his way out.

"Can I talk to you a minute, Marshal?" Sam asked, filling the door.

"If it's short and quick. I'm on my way down to Olathe to hang a man."

"That's no reason to hurry." Sam smiled and went on into the office.

"They complain if you're late," the tobacco-chewing marshal said. "Like you're just as bad as everybody else in his life because you broke your promise to hang him at noon sharp, and he's had to wait around a half hour twiddlin' his thumbs and playin' mumblety-peg."

"Short and quick. I'd like to know about whatever men been killed in the past six months."

"My territory only goes to Salina," the marshal said, putting on his coat. "That good enough?"

"No, I don't reckon," Sam said, losing his smile. "I know he's dead—or I'm pretty sure, but I don't know where at."

"What was his name?"

"Faraday, but he might have changed it to Greer."

"Nothin' comes to mind," the marshal said, buckling on his six-gun. "Anything alse?"

"He had a wooden hand and white hair."

"Now, that does ring a bell," the marshal said, putting his peaked hat on, "but I can't place it. Had somethin' to do with a robbery in Louisiana some years back . . ."

"Could you pin it down some more?"

"Only thing I remember is that part about the white

hair and the wooden hand," the marshal said, heading for the door. "If I get an idea, I'll tell you when I get back."

Trudging over to Ma Krenkel's rooming house, Sam had the notion someone was following him, but each time he tried a ruse to test his concern, no one appeared.

Worryin' too much, he thought. Why would anybody want to follow me? I ain't goin' nowhere, been nowhere, and I'm headed for a place where nowhere runs into nothin'.

It being midday, Sam was able to soak in the copper tub awhile extra to get the kinks out of his neck and his good humor restored.

Billy, Billy—the refrain ran through Sam's mind— where are you? Why are you sending strange messages to me? Why don't you just come and set awhile?

"Cause you're not able to travel."

Something almighty bad is holdin' you back—like about six feet of dirt.

Dressed in a clean outfit and freshly shaved, he felt ten years younger and a fine hunger in his midsection.

Ira's Lunch was large enough to provide a counter with ten stools, as well as room for six tables and chairs to match. Ira's wife, Melba, bossed the kitchen while Ira pegged around on his crutch, greeting the customers, taking their orders, and generally enjoying himself. He'd lost the leg at Sharpsburg, which forever altered his conversation afterward because it marked the end and beginning of Ira's life.

Ever since Sharpsburg . . . Before Sharpsburg . . . Up until Sharpsburg . . . Wasn't until Sharpsburg . . .

"Howdy there, Sam." Ira pegged forward to shake hands. "You're lookin' fit and fancy as a calf in a posy patch."

"How's the roast beef holdin' up?"

"Melba, sweetie, got a hungry man here wants heap beef!" Ira called back into the kitchen as Sam took a seat at the counter.

"Where's old Skofer?" Ira asked. "You goin' to let him starve to death?"

"He's got a new job," Sam said.

"That's kinda hard to believe." Ira smiled. "Not to call you a liar, but what can he do?"

"He's givin' voice lessons. Teachin' singin'."

"Ain't the world wonderful! There's a place for everyone." Ira chuckled happily and pegged off to the cash box to make change for a customer.

From the kitchen came a new waitress carrying a platter, and it took Sam a second to place her as Elizabeth Faraday because she was dressed in a clean, stylish frock and a crisp apron, and her hair had been piled up in a bun.

"Ah, Mr. Benbow," she said, unsmiling. "Roast beef and the trimmings?"

"That's right the first time, Miss Faraday—or is it Mrs. Armenescu?" Sam replied neutrally, the sense of fun going out of the room.

Placing the platter crowded with crispy roast beef, mashed potatoes covered with rich brown gravy, boiled squash, onions, and coleslaw before Sam, she asked, "How did you find out about Rene?"

"It wasn't easy." Sam piled the mashed potatoes on his fork and took a healthy bite. "Congratulations to the cook." He smiled.

"Tell me," she said nervously.

"Your man here in Topeka?"

"Anything else, Mr. Benbow?" she asked stiffly, stepping back.

"A piece of apple pie later on, and maybe a hunk of rat cheese piled on top."

As she started back to the kitchen, Sam added, "I

don't blame you none for clearing out of that kingdom of increase."

She stared at him, her eyes seeking his. "You know it?"

"Been there and back." Sam didn't pause in packing in his dinner.

"And Dad?"

"I'm workin' on it."

"Elizabeth, order's ready!" Melba called from the kitchen.

"I'll come to your office later," Elizabeth said, hurrying back into the kitchen.

Without paying attention to the comings and goings of the other customers, Sam settled down to enjoying the tasty dinner.

Savoring the richly crusted roast beef, he felt an annoyance as he smelled a cheap perfume coming from close by, and thinking it was a woman who had elected to sit beside him, he glanced over and saw a dark-skinned man with oiled curly black hair, dressed in a striped suit that Sam thought might have come from a prison for high-class politicians.

"You're Sam Benbow?" the oily stranger purred in an accent strange to Sam's ears, until he remembered the patois of New Orleans.

"And you must be Rene Armenescu." Sam nodded, trying the coleslaw flavored with chopped black walnuts.

"You know me?"

"I'm not tryin' too hard."

"Always the joke!" Armenescu retorted like a challenge.

"Mmmm . . ." Sam murmured, trying the buttered squash with cinnamon and nutmeg sprinkled on it.

"I see you talk to my fiancée," Armenescu said with a warning in his voice.

"She works here," Sam said.

"You can order without upsetting her with your advances."

"Mister, you're smellin' around the butt of the wrong hound dog," Sam said mildly.

"I'm not afraid. What do you want?"

"I'd appreciate it if you'd move downwind."

"Always the smart talk from the western gunfighter," Armenescu sneered.

Putting his fork down on the platter and anchoring it in the mashed potatoes, Sam swung a hard backhand into the swarthy man's face with such snapping force, it knocked him off the stool.

"That's better." Sam picked up his fork and tried the dilled salt beans.

"You cannot do this to me!" Armenescu got to his feet, addressing Sam's back.

Sam cut into the rare heart of the beef and nodded his head with approval, ignoring Armenescu, who stormed out the front door.

Ira pegged back from the cash box. "What's goin' on here?"

"Nothin' much, Ira. You know how it is when I talk with my hands. Always flingin' around, makin' trouble for myself."

Glancing over to his right, Sam saw Elizabeth standing in the doorway, a worried expression on her face.

"Don't worry, ma'am," Sam said, "your man is a fast learner."

"He's just a friend," she said simply. I didn't know he was so jealous."

"Has every right to be," Sam said gallantly, swabbing up the remaining gravy with a piece of sourdough bread, and pushing the empty platter away. "What line of work is he in?"

"He's studying the law," Elizabeth said, taking the platter and going back to the kitchen.

When Elizabeth returned with a big wedge of apple pie with sugared brown crust topped by a slab of golden cheese, the front door opened for the banker and a man Sam didn't know, although he noticed immediately the six-shooter tied down to the tall man's leg. Behind them, lagging back, came Skofer himself, his washed-out blue eyes looking everywhere but at Sam as he sat down alongside.

"Afternoon, Cap'n," he said in a small voice.

"This is the busiest place in town. Everybody's comin' or goin'," Sam said neutrally.

"I've been looking for you, Cap'n."

"Urgent business?"

"Not exactly, but you never know."

"Never know what?"

"When."

"When what?"

"Where, then."

"What, where, when then?"

"Sam," Skofer sputtered, "be serious!"

"Seriously, Skofer, if we ever get a place of our own, we're goin' to name it Apple Pie Ranch."

"I rather thought we'd call it home sweet home," Skofer said, his thin face serious, his mouth set determinedly, as if he were ready to go out and fight for the dream.

"Seen Rip around lately?" Sam asked.

Skofer's eyes shifted about wildly until he could find his voice. "No, not lately."

"Happen to remember little Billy Faraday back when?"

"Course I remember, Cap'n. Always dashing around in a great style."

"Had that long, pretty feather tucked in his hat—

always lifted the hearts of the barefooted fighting men."

"And had more guts than you could hang on a fence. You're rambling on about little Billy. . . . Have you seen him?"

"Kind of hold your high notes down some, Skofe," Sam murmured. "That banker and his friend seemed to be leaning this way like they was a strong wind against 'em."

"You hear from him?" Skofer whispered.

Sam nodded almost imperceptibly.

"That's why you've been gallivanting around the country?"

"You about ready to sacrifice your opera career for some hard, dangerous, low-payin' work?"

Skofer swallowed twice, his prominent Adam's apple bobbing up and down his stringy neck.

"I guess I could spare the time," he croaked.

"Fine. We got some little business to attend to," Sam said as Elizabeth came out again, this time carrying a large, blue-enameled coffeepot. Sam looked up into her face and saw that she had been crying. Such a beautiful and lost face, he thought, and said, "I'm workin' on it, ma'am; don't let it get too rainy."

She gave him a quick look of gratitude.

"There's so much—" she said, not finishing as the banker Sark tapped his glass loudly and said, "May we have some service, lady?"

"Certainly." She nodded and hurried to take the order.

"That'll be fifty cents, Sam," old Ira said.

Sam, just for the hell of it, flipped the new twenty-dollar gold piece on the counter and glanced sidewise at Elijah Sark.

He saw the meechy mouth pucker up, eyes blink, the soft hands tremble.

As Sam pulled back the coin and laid out half a dollar, he looked into the eyes of the man with the tied-down gun and saw a man he would sooner or later have to fight. A younger man, maybe in better shape, maybe faster on the draw and keener with the first shot. It was all there in the gray, icy eyes staring back at him, mocking him.

4

Sylvan Grove, having finished with the roosters about town challenging one another's dominions, seemed to lie brooding as the prairie wind sang its sad threnody over the vast plains, empty except for the few gritty sodbusters living in their dugouts and soddies out in the lonely.

There wasn't a red or yellow shirt in town. If it wasn't dark blue, it was gray or black.

The women favored gray dresses, except for those who had only their funeral clothes left to wear.

It was a poor little town with few prospects. The lawyer and the saloonkeeper thought if they could steal the county seat from Arboreal Splendor, they'd all prosper and the railroad might send up a spur, but the last time they'd tried to seize the county records and hold a vote, the blacksmith had been killed by a loyal Arboreal Splendor patriot with a saber left over from the war, and there was no hope of mounting another attack for a while. With little else to do except to find shelter from the wind, the various townsmen gathered in the saloon and discussed what they should do about the property of the late Bill Greer.

"We've discovered no will," lawyer Ogden Santee said. He wasn't a certified lawyer, but he'd once sold apples in the courthouse down at Blue Cascades, and he'd learned a lot there.

"Seems to me all his goods should go to the city of Sylvan Grove then," Cornelius Van der Luen said. "I could use the forge and vise."

"Not so fast," Abe Freels said. "If we're going to take it all, we'll share it even steven amongst us."

"That's fair," Lonnie Hubbard said, "but I'd sort of like to set claim to his six-gun."

"Let's take a look and put it to a vote," Santee said.

In this way the group of a dozen loyal and true citizens of Sylvan Grove arrived in buckboards and wagons at the residence of the late Uncle Billy Greer.

They hurried and jostled one another as they stampeded toward the gate in the picket fence, hammers, crowbars, gunnysacks, and bushel baskets in their hands.

Mrs. Darmody had brought a willow wand cage for Uncle Billy's Dominecker hens, which he'd always cared for as if they were his family.

Her neighbor, Mrs. Peabody, and her husband the Reverend Arthur Peabody carried a steamer trunk between them, ready to load up blankets, curtains, carpets, and the better articles of clothing.

Ogden Santee, too small to fight much, had two wooden crates that he intended to fill with Uncle Billy's books, because no one else wanted them.

An enthusiastic and hateful mob, they elbowed one another for first place to the gate when they were met by a stocky, redheaded lady holding Billy's repeating

.44–40 rifle, its octagonal barrel pointed in general at the leader of the committee, Ogden Santee.

"That's as far as you're goin'!" the red-haired lady declared before the gate could open.

"Now, now, Ruby . . ." Santee called out. "We've decided Mr. Greer's goods belong to the city of Sylvan Grove, and that's all there is to it."

"Off with you, you mealymouthed spalpeen!"

Mrs. O'Banion, a handsome thirty-year-old woman who, if you counted Uncle Billy, had buried three husbands already, stood fast. "You'll take none of Billy's goods."

"You don't have a choice," Lonnie Hubbard declared, backing away as Ruby swung the rifle barrel toward him.

"Faith and I've got the choice right here. You know Billy was mine, and what he left is mine."

"He left no will. You're not even married," the minister Peabody said piously.

"He said he couldn't marry, but we was as good as wed anyways, not that any of you haven't gossiped enough about it," Ruby O'Banion said firmly.

"You have no right—" Sol Burns croaked like crow with the croup.

"I loved him, and I buried him, bless his soul. That's my right, and Mr. Winchester—sure and he gives me a right, too."

"You'll regret this, you Jezebel," Mrs. Darmody yelled.

"Get out, you thievin' hypocrites—" Ruby O'Banion's freckled face flushed red "—or I'm fixin' to shoot!"

The committee moved back.

"You'll never be able to live with us," Ogden Santee piped up.

"That's what I want," she replied. "The first immigrant that's crazy enough to want to live in this town, I'm goin' to sell out to, and if you trouble me more about it, you'll find out what a mad Irishwoman looks like!"

The group drifted away, murmuring imprecations and hollow songs of sorrow at her bereavement, but she stood firmly at the gate until the last of them were gone.

Backing up to the little house, she sat on the front steps, put her face in the crook of her arm, and wept.

After a few minutes she collected herself and went inside, where, as an occasional housekeeper, she'd seen that everything was neat and tidy to Billy's taste, but not so regimented that he felt uncomfortable.

All he had wanted was peace and quiet, his workshop, his books, his pipe, a glass of Kentucky whiskey, a fried chicken dinner once a week. Not much. But the little things were precious to him, and she'd done her best to abide by his wishes, staying out of the way most times unless he needed her, and then she came to him willingly. She'd darned his socks and washed his clothes. She'd beat the carpets and cooked his dinner and gone to his bed. Who else in this damned scraggly town had cared so much for him?

"Ah, Billy . . . ah, my Billy . . ." She remembered the lines of pain and grief in his face and eyes. "You knew all along the devil was on your back, didn't you?"

Gazing about the unpretentious living room where Billy spent most of his evenings, she saw his plew of Carroll's Lone Jack tobacco, near the old calfskin-bound copies of *The Spectator,* which he enjoyed reading over and over, as well as his black leather-bound Bible, which he sometimes would read aloud because he said the words made a special kind of music. There were his soft gaiters that he liked to wear around the house. Hanging on the wall was a cavalry saber and a battered kossuth hat with a bedraggled remnant of a feather in its band.

She sat down in his chair and leaned back. When he'd first come to Sylvan Grove and roomed at the Windsor Arms until he'd made up his mind he wanted to stay, everyone wondered what he'd done or meant to do. They poked around, asking pointed questions, made deductions, tried to fit him into a safe pigeon-hole. Yet he'd always answered in vague terms, almost childlike, giving simple answers that meant next to nothing.

"How'd you lose your hand?"

"Doctor took it off."

"Why?"

"It didn't work anymore."

"What happened to it?"

"They buried it or give it to the dogs. I don't rightly know."

"I mean, why did they cut it off?"

"It didn't work anymore."

Round and round they'd gone, like a pack of mutts testing a new arrival. No one wanted to try fighting him because he wore the blue Colt like he knew it pretty well, and you couldn't really feel good about pushing a crippled man around.

Of course, Abe Freels had to try something. He couldn't have been the town bully otherwise. He'd claimed Billy had bumped him in the Red Rose Card Parlor and tried to back Billy up for it—kind of slapped Billy's face just to show he was the rooster on the high perch—and Billy had brought that wooden hand around and knocked Abe Freels nine ways from Sunday. They said you could hear that chunk of wood smack Freels's jaw a block away. . . .

They said his eyes were ablazin' like blue lightning on a stormy night. . . .

Sure now, Freels nor anybody else cared to crowd him after that. They just settled into the daily routine.

She sighed. When she'd gotten word that her father was dying and she had nothing saved up from taking in washing, Billy went over toward Ellsworth soon as he heard about it, and when he came back, he put five hundred dollars in her apron, and said, "You go on home and see your dad off."

When she returned, she'd kind of wanted to pay him back, but he said, no, that wasn't in the bargain.

Then about a week later she had come over of an evening and found him sitting in the big chair reading by the lamp, smoking his pipe. She'd knelt down beside him, put her head on his knee, and said, "Billy, I want to."

Later, he'd slept so badly it worried her, making tight little shrieks—as if he were warnin' somebody in battle. His body would twist and convulse as if he were fightin' a nine-headed dragon. She'd held him until he calmed down.

And that was why he always looked so worn with pain and sorrow. It was more than his hand. It was too many battles for one small boy to carry. Not just losing his wife and daughter, it was too much blood and too many broken bones. Too many screams of the maimed and blinded. Too many horses running by, dragging their guts. Too many mass graves. Too many houses burned. Too many blood brethren slaughtered on the killing ground.

As she thought back over what she knew about Billy Greer, she felt as if something just wasn't meshing together right. Billy never worked, except on his inventions, and though he won a few pennies playing poker, he couldn't have lived so well on that. Everyone just assumed he was living off his pension, but somehow it didn't wash. Looking at the insignia on the hat and saber, she suddenly realized he couldn't have gotten any pension at all, because he'd not fought for the North like everyone thought. He'd fought on the side of the Confederacy.

Somehow he'd let people believe what they wanted to believe. Everyone had thought his soft drawl was from one of the border states, Tennessee or West Virginia, but the sword, sure as shooting, had a brass boss on its hilt that said CSA on it.

That meant he had no pension. No support. Of course, every month he rode over to Ellsworth and came back with his month's money. It could be he had his mail coming there and somebody back home was sending him the money. Yet it didn't make sense. The weekly mail came up to Sylvan Grove from the Arboreal Splendor post office. If he was to get any mail, it would come that way.

She shivered uncontrollably as she realized the danger of her thinking. Best forget it.

Somebody out there was a brutal killer. Some evil person had tracked Billy down and . . .

Sure! Of course! Suddenly it all made sense. Billy had settled down in Sylvan Grove because he was trying to hide. In such a backwater town on the long prairie, a man could seem to have disappeared off the face of the earth if he walked softly and minded his own business.

Was he hiding from someone he'd hurt in the war?

No. Sure not, silly, she told herself, seeing the pieces coming together. It was the money. Someone wanted Billy's money.

Why hadn't they come on over and dug it up?

Because Billy didn't tell them where he lived. Or maybe he lied and told them he lived down at Vesper or Shady Bend.

It all added up in her mind. Billy had a big sack of money that somebody knew about. That somebody had finally run him down and tortured him to death without learning where it was.

Then where was it?

It had to be right here in this little house, maybe buried outside, or in the shed—someplace close where he could keep an eye on it.

Again she trembled with fear. She knew too much. If that somebody ever found out she was friends with Billy . . .

At that moment she wished she were back in Chicago, where she knew she could handle the neighborhood toughs. Out here, it was different. It was so big, you couldn't watch all the ratholes.

Now, if she were that somebody . . . she would be traveling from town to town, asking if there was a man named Billy Greer lived here until she found the right town. . . .

Yet no strangers had come through Sylvan Grove since his death, not even his daughter, so maybe Billy had fooled them some other way.

Having cleaned house and washed clothes for Billy for over a year, she couldn't believe there was anything in the little house she didn't know about.

Course, it could be buried in the storm cellar or out back in the garden, or maybe there was a secret compartment he'd built in back of a cupboard or something. . . .

Saints and snakes, she thought. Billy, what a burden you have laid on me! Maybe I'm rich, maybe I'm poor, it don't make a nevermind, because sure as spuds, someone is comin' after me!

Well, scat, girl! If they're goin' to burn you, better you find that money and get to movin' to parts unknown!

"What are we lookin' for, Cap'n?" Skofer asked as they walked down the street.

"I don't know," Sam admitted. "We've got a case. It starts with this gold piece."

"Let me look at that." Skofer held out his hand. "I don't suppose you knew I was once a famous numismatist?"

"Is that a penal offense or just a misdemeanor?" Sam asked, as Skofer stopped to examine the coin.

"New Orleans. Three years back."

"If that's all it takes to be a thing like you're famous for, I reckon I'm at the head of the class."

"Tell you something else . . ." Skofer scratched his stubbly chin. "Sure is unusual."

"How do you mean?"

"The first eagles were struck in 1795. They were called eagles because they always had that bird on the reverse side, and they were worth ten dollars."

"So a double eagle is worth twenty dollars," Sam nodded.

"The first double eagles were struck in 1849, and they all have the eagle on the reverse, and the goddess of Liberty on the front," Skofer said.

"What else, Professor?" Sam asked respectfully.

"Last double eagles minted in New Orleans was 1861. Right before the war. They haven't made any twenty-dollar pieces since then. Maybe it's the only one ever made. Seems real, though."

Sam took the coin back. "So what do we know now that we didn't before we bought your expert opinion?"

"Simply that it's a rare piece. Never been out, nor is it in any book or circular."

"How can that be?" Sam asked seriously.

"Either the whole issue was melted down again because of something wrong with it, or else they were stored in the basement of the mint where some high-priced clerk forgot about it."

"Suppose the whole batch could have been stolen?"

"I'd think there'd be some circulating." Skofer shook his head. "No, they've been hidden out by accident or design."

"I'm spinnin' a yarn around in my head. I know Billy Faraday left Veitengruber, Missouri, and turned up in Louisiana. This coin was stamped New Orleans."

"I can't see that lad holding up a U.S. mint." Skofer shook his head.

Sam put the coin back in his vest pocket and considered the possibilities.

"How come a heavyweight pug came after me in Missouri?" he asked himself out loud.

"You never tell me anything," Skofer complained. "Why didn't you take me along? I'd have beaten him to flinderjigs."

"Seems you were showin' folks how to kiss a mule's butt and still survive, and I just didn't want to interfere in the exhibition."

"No, that was last week."

"It was somethin' along that line, I suppose," Sam said mildly. "Maybe you was buried in the theories of that bird Darwin, or considering why grass is green. I don't recollect."

"Now you're being downright petty," Skofer protested, pausing before the swinging batwing doors of Sullivan's Tavern and Oyster Emporium. "After all this talking, I'm feeling kind of dry. Aren't you?"

"I just finished my dinner, Skofe." Sam grinned. "But I reckon I could watch you drink a beer."

"We don't want to spend that gold piece," Skofer said, worried.

"I'm not spendin' anything. I'm just watchin', remember?"

"Well . . . I'm a touch short today, but my remittance from Norway should be here tomorrow," Skofer said seriously.

"You mean can I stake you till your remittance comes?"

"It's just a matter of a day or two." Skofer licked his thin, dry lips and rolled his eyes around nervously.

"Likely you'd have a fit right here on the sidewalk was I to say no." Sam grinned.

Skofer led the way, almost at an indecent trot, aiming for the portly magnificence of Sullivan himself, who, having seen the small bed slat of a man come in the door, was already drawing a beer from the spigot.

"You know I can't think straight without a cold glass of beer in my hand," Skofer said, draining the stein and sliding it back to Sullivan.

"I'm inclined to agree. You sure don't solve any of my problems dry." Sam nodded to Sullivan, who drew another beer and placed it in front of the former professor.

"You start howlin'," Sullivan growled, "I'm goin' to send you to the vet for a operation that'll make you a soprano."

Skofer looked at Sullivan out of the corner of his eye, then looked at the glass of beer, then muttered, "Maybe it'd be worth it."

Sullivan laughed and moved down the bar to serve a pair of legislators who had the ability to look serious and jolly at the same time. "How's the wonderful war going?" "We're losing all our men, but we're winning for their own good. . . ."

"Let's get serious now that my stomach knows my throat's not cut," Skofer said, fingering the stubble on his pointed chin, compressing his thin, rubbery lips.

"That ain't like you," Sam said.

"No more drollery, Cap'n. We have a problem of significant proportions."

"There's more fancy words in that glass of beer than in Webster's latest lexicon." Sam smiled.

"There's the evidence in your pocket, but by all accounts, it doesn't even exist. It came from Billy Faraday to his daughter, who hardly remembers him."

"She remembers some. She remembers how his hair had turned white, and the wooden hand with the glove on it. She remembers—"

"Hold it there just a moment, Cap'n!" Skofer held up his small, scrawny hand. "I recollect none of that myself."

"Ah, damn!" Sam frowned. "Of course. You were invalided out a year early. What the hell was it you had? Poison ivy or monster lice—something you incurred in the line of duty?"

"Cap'n, please . . ." Skofer blushed. "Whatever it was, I haven't got it now."

"That's it, now I recall—"

"Please don't recall, Cap'n."

"There was them dusky maidens offering eternal love for a sack of corn or something. . . ."

"Rolled oats," Skofer croaked, his eyes rolling upward.

"And so you went to Texas to recover—"

"It was a hard trip. I wasn't so lucky as some I know."

Sam's laughter boomed through the room, and he hugged the diminutive old man close for a moment, "Lucky! Yes, indeedy! We're here!"

"Now, what were you leading up to before you started making sport of your old comrade in arms?" Skofer stood straighter and signaled Sullivan with one finger for another beer.

"I was sayin' you left the party early. And you didn't ever see Billy afterward."

"He was a dashing, gallant lad!" Skofer saluted the memory with his stein.

"Not after Chickamauga. He lost his hand. His hair turned white, and he became almighty quiet, like he was so full of pain and hell, he'd never smile again."

"Lost his hand?"

"Another inch, it'd been his whole arm." Sam nodded.

"One of the boys carved him a hand out of soft pine, and then he went off to Veitengruber, Missouri, to get his butt kicked real hard."

"Now, Cap'n . . ." Skofer's eyes lighted, and a little smile tugged at the corner of his mouth. "Now I'm going to show you what a few beers are worth. I will now tell you where that twenty-dollar gold piece came from."

"Take your time, Skofe. How about as soon as you can get that one down?"

"Some years back," Skofer said ponderously, "I was perusing *Harper's Monthly,* and—"

"Perusing?" Sam smiled.

"Well, if you're going to be that way, I'll go tell the banker or somebody. . . ."

"One more, Tim!" Sam called down the bar.

"There was an interesting article about a mystery man murdering a woman who worked in the New Orleans Mint."

"Oh, no, dammit!" Sam said, gritting his teeth.

"A white-haired man who looked old but strong,

57

with a wooden left hand, just walked into the mint one night and shot the poor lady dead, then he ran off and disappeared before anyone could catch him."

"You've put some pieces together," Sam said, "but they don't make sense. I know that Billy Faraday would never shoot a woman. He was always busy defendin' women."

"I remember," Skofer said, "but that is the story, and I am not making up a word of it."

"Have you still got that *Harper's Monthly?*"

"Perhaps I threw it away, but if you like, we can take a look in my quarters, Cap'n."

"I'd like to very much, if you think you can make it clear down to Ma Krenkel's roomin' house by now."

"My boy," Skofer smiled, "I may choose to fly."

In a somewhat precarious fashion they made their way down the walk to the rooming house, where Skofer asked permission from the landlady to visit the attic of the commodious Victorian mansion.

"So long as Sam is with you . . ." Ma Krenkel agreed reluctantly, seeing the unsteady step and moist eyes of the little man.

After climbing three flights of stairs, Skofer was out of breath and pale of face, and Sam was wondering if he'd make it all the way.

Getting his breath back, Skofer went on to a round turret sun room that gave a vista of the whole of Topeka, Kansas, including a large stretch of the river and the railroad tracks.

Skofer swallowed dryly and said, "If you hadn't saved my life at Manassas, I'd think twice about going to such lengths to help your cause."

"Seems like I saved your life twice at Manassas," Sam said.

"I try to forget the horror of those days." Skofer

smiled mockingly, and went on into the full-sized attic.

Amongst wicker hampers, cowhide chests, and broken furniture were boxes of books and periodicals.

"These yours?" Sam asked.

"I don't know why I hang on to them." Skofer nodded and sat down alongside a pile of *Harper's Monthly*s bound together with twine. "We're talking about three years ago, I'd guess. . . ." Skofer sorted through the bundles until he found the right year.

After undoing the twine, he riffled through each magazine, mostly made up of ladies' fashions, kitchen advice, a serial romance, and perhaps an article of contemporary interest.

"Got it!" he said, as if he'd just caught a big fish on a small hook. Folding the March 1879 issue of the magazine open, he gave it to Sam, pointing at the title.

MYSTERY MAN MURDERS MINT SUPERVISOR
IN COLD BLOOD

An engraved plate showed a leering monster of a man firing a smoking revolver at short range into the breast of a beautiful woman.

Sam turned the magazine to the light.

Apparently for no motive whatsoever, Mrs. Carl Utter, administrative supervisor at the New Orleans mint, was murdered by an unknown assailant described as a strong elderly man with white hair, burning eyes, and a false left hand covered by a black glove.

Jason Bacon, guard at the mint, reported that he heard the fatal shot, and was forced to take cover by the fusillade of shots fired at him as the killer escaped by a side door.

Arnold Beane, specie inventory accountant under Mrs. Utter's supervision, has reported that nothing is missing.

Authorities admit they have no clues and can only conclude that the white-haired man with the dead hand murdered the woman through mistaken identity.

Sam returned the magazine to Skofer. "It still doesn't make sense. Billy would never murder a woman, not even the worst poxed hellcat that ever lived."

"Would you agree that he fits the description?"

"Yes, he fits it, but there's probably a lot more, too."

"It's all tied together with that coin in your vest pocket," Skofer said seriously. "I'm not saying Billy did it. I'm saying it's as logical as the theory of Copernicus."

"All right," Sam said, "someone used him."

"Now that I've set you on the right path, let us retire to the nearest social parlor for invigoration." Skofer tied the bundle back together, making a tidy mound of the dusty magazines.

As they were passing over the gleaming parquet floor of the parlor on the ground floor, Ma Krenkel called to them from the kitchen. "Did your cousin find you, Mr. Benbow?"

"Cousin?" Sam asked, turning back and going to the open door where Ma Krenkel was extracting the entrails from a plump chicken, carefully setting the gizzard, liver, and heart aside.

"What cousin?"

"George, he said. George Brown. Had a face mashed up like a Hubbard squash. I told him you were in the attic, and he said he'd just like to say hello—"

Sam was already running back up the stairs, down the hall, and into his unlocked room.

The double featherbed had been thrown aside, blankets scattered about wildly.

"By the Bard, Sam, what's going on!" Skofer exclaimed, coming in a minute later.

"Somebody's itemized my personal belongings," Sam said tightly. "There wasn't anything in here worth stealin'."

"Curious, your cousin George Brown."

"I know an hombre with a face that looks like a Hubbard squash, except he's bigger and meaner." Sam shook his head angrily. "And when I catch up with him, I'm goin' to mash him up some and stuff him with sausage and onions."

5

Sam Benbow ran up the steps three at a time, hoping against hope that what he expected hadn't happened.

Charging down the corridor, he found the door to his office hanging by one hinge, the lock broken, the jamb splintered.

"Goddammit!" he growled. "It wasn't even locked."

"Looks like a herd of buffalos went through," Skofer said, following Sam inside.

The desk drawers were scattered about on the floor, the pigeonholes emptied, along with the scanty files he kept for the Stockman's Association. Even his spare bottle of Kentucky bourbon had been smashed against the wall.

After searching through the various papers, Sam sighed and shook his head. "Not here."

"What are we searching for, Cap'n?" Skofer asked in a small voice.

"We are lookin' for the two notes that Elizabeth

Faraday put in my trust," Sam replied, smacking his big hands together in frustration. "I just didn't think they were important enough to steal."

"But who is interested?" Skofer asked.

"That big orangutan, my cousin George Brown."

"The next question is why?"

"When I have the answer to that, I'm goin' to be rappin' somebody on the head." Sam snorted, thoroughly disgusted with himself.

"What was so important in the letter?"

"Nothing. Something about how it wasn't the first nor the last when the chickens came home to roost, and that I'd likely want to make things right."

"The envelope?"

"Wasn't any."

"No way to tell where it came from?"

"No. The lady that sent it didn't put her address on it. Her name was O'Banion. Ruby O'Banion."

"So Mr. Somebody knows three names. Elizabeth's, Ruby's, and yours."

"But he only knows where I am."

"Can't Elizabeth be connected?"

"It's hardly possible. She's going under her real name, and Billy changed his to Greer."

"Mr. Somebody is awfully close to all of us," Skofer worried.

"Skofe, do me a favor. Poke around a little without gettin' yourself killed and see what you can find out."

"I know where to start, Cap'n." Skofer stood at attention, but Sam turned away before he could salute too.

Elizabeth Faraday finished washing the supper dishes while Melba set the dough for the next day's bread, and Ira worked over the day's accounts.

"Go to bed, child," Melba, a large lady with a weakness for her own cooking, said. "It's been a long day."

"I don't mind," Elizabeth replied, drying her hands on her apron. "I like to keep busy, so long as I feel I'm doing something worth the doing."

"Good night, Elizabeth," old Ira said, looking up from the ledger. "Don't let the fleas tickle your knees."

"I'll try not to." She smiled and went out into the gathering dusk.

Seeing Rene Armenescu waiting on the boardwalk, she frowned with disappointment. Somehow in her heart she had hoped that big Sam Benbow might be there instead.

She'd been a little overwhelmed by the dazzling Latin splendor of Rene when he'd first stopped at the Veitengruber farm. He had talked excitedly about the bright future in Topeka, how he intended to be a lawyer, how someday he'd run for governor, and he spoke with such sincere enthusiasm, you couldn't help believing him.

But there'd been a tiny change, a minute crack in the image of the handsome young man, when he'd asked to borrow a small amount of money to buy some medicine he needed.

Then she had noticed his hair tonic had become more like roses instead of lilac, and it entered her mind that her little bit of money had gone to pay for just a different perfume.

Such a small thing it was, and yet once the doubt was started, her faith in him and his future plans was diminished.

She believed him when he told her he was spending his time reading the law with a local lawyer. Of course, he couldn't make ends meet as a student, yet he managed to dress more elegantly than most of the men who came in the restaurant, with his yellow silk four-in-hand and frock coat lined with red sateen.

He had hinted at marriage, but she had not given him any kind of encouragement, thinking it was much too soon to be so serious, and yet lately, he'd taken to calling her his fiancée, and getting mighty smooth with his hands, touching her here and there as if she'd given herself to him already.

Indeed, wholesomely tired as she felt, she was not pleased to see him standing in the gloom.

"Hello, my little sweetheart!" Armenescu stepped forward, his white teeth shining in his dark, handsome features.

"Hello, Rene." She sidestepped quickly so that his encircling arm missed and a momentary expression of fury flashed over his face.

"May I walk with you, my dear?" He recovered his composure and bowed.

"I'm going straight around to my room."

"How much better if we could ride a golden surrey to the Vanderbilt Arms," he said lightly, walking beside her.

She thought she smelled a different perfume in his black, shining curls, something disagreeable like narcissus.

"It's been a long day," she said simply.

"You work too hard for too little money," he declared.

"The Armsburys were good enough to let me live in the spare room and pay me a good wage besides. I'm not complaining. They're decent, and they don't try to run my life for me."

"Have you ever thought of going on the stage?"

"Me? Frogs sing sweeter'n me." She smiled.

"Perhaps, but there is not a more beautiful woman

in the entire state if you would learn the proper presentation."

"What kind of a presentation is proper?" she asked. "You don't like my gingham?"

"I would like to see you in a silken gown, trimmed with gold braid, wearing long white gloves, gliding about a polished floor."

"That's a horse of a different color," she said, not exactly sincerely, because she felt thrilled by the flattery and the vision of herself dressed in the latest fashion, like one of the wives of the profiteers who had emerged from the bones of the Civil War like toadstools—arrogant, vain, fatuous, and immensely rich.

"I could be your agent," he said, smiling, "and we'd both become rich."

"No, Rene," she said seriously. "Those folks over at Veitengruber don't teach their young ones singing or dancing. They teach 'em how to pitch hay and milk cows."

"Your beauty is too overpowering to be wasted on just me," he said. "It's not hard to learn how to entertain an audience of well-wishers, and there's great deal of money in it. You could be independently wealthy overnight."

"Right now, Rene, all I want is to get a good night's sleep," she said, coming to the back door of the restaurant.

"I wish you would permit me to be of some service to you, my dear," Rene said softly, taking her strong hands in his own.

"Find my father, Rene. That's something I really want," she said impulsively.

"He's lost?" Rene asked sympathetically.

"He may be dead. I wish I knew."

"Why is he so hard to find?"

"I don't know. All I know is he changed his name to Greer and changed his life after he left Veitengruber."

"Interesting that he would change his name. Did he commit a crime?" Armenescu asked smoothly, his mind alert.

After saying that much, she had to tell about the letter from Mrs. O'Banion, her finding Sam Benbow here in town, and the twenty-dollar gold piece.

"I will speak to my lawyer friend about this," Armenescu encouraged her. "Is there anything else?"

"No, that's the trouble. I don't know anything!" she cried out, her weariness robbing her of caution. "Sam Benbow just goes around wasting time and telling me nothing."

"I will get to the bottom of this, my dear one," Armenescu said, putting his arms around her waist, drawing her close.

She smelled the punky perfume of narcissus and backed away.

"I don't know what got into me. I'm talkin' like a hysterical schoolgirl that's just stepped on a garter snake."

"Don't worry about a thing," Rene said smoothly. "I'll take personal charge."

"Don't do anything, Rene," she said earnestly. "And don't say anything. Forget I ever mentioned it."

"Good night, my sweet," he said, bowing, and withdrawing into the darkness.

"That woman has to be here in town!" Banker Elijah Sark banged his desktop for emphasis. "We've got to find her. She's our link to this Mrs. O'Banion."

Weed studied the letters and shook his head. "There's too many people coming and going in this town. It's practically a city, and you don't know if her name is Greer or Veitengruber or Faraday."

"It doesn't make any difference. We ask for all of them. They're uncommon names."

"Ask who?" Bull Basham asked. "All the ladies goin' down the street with their shopping baskets?"

"No. The rooming houses, of course," Sark said bitterly. "We've got to move faster than Benbow can think."

"I'll knock that Benbow on his butt next time I see him." Bull Basham grinned, revealing his broken teeth.

"Not Benbow," Weed said. "He's nothin'. Sark is right about the connection."

"I can ask around," Bull Basham said. "It'd be a lot easier if you'd tell me what it's all about, though."

"Find her!" Sark almost screamed with frustration and rage. "We are so close, and yet so far!"

"And so is Benbow," Weed sneered. "Only, he knows who she is and we don't."

"Can you kill him?" Sark asked plain out.

"In a fair fight?"

"I don't care how you do it," the banker growled. "Can you?"

"I can put his lights out from the front or the back, it don't make any difference." Weed nodded. "Just tell me when."

"Not yet, but be ready. If he finds the connection between us and the gold piece, he's too dangerous to live."

Bull Basham's gimlet eyes glinted brightly for a second, as it dawned on him these two men had been looking for the man Greer for over three years and that it was now a matter of life or death to them.

That meant there was either a lot of money out there somewhere or evidence of murder, or both.

"I better get busy," Bull Basham muttered, clambering to his feet and putting on his derby.

Basham had no idea of actually convassing all the rooming houses, boardinghouses, hotels, or homes with rooms for rent. There were just too many people coming through town on their way west, as Weed had said, to try to find any one person out of the mob.

Heading down East Sixth Avenue, all Basham wanted was to rub shoulders with people he understood. Ex-pugs, pool sharks, promoters, shysters, opportunists on the edge of the law, easy women, and a good time.

Cherry Avenue across the tracks was a special neighborhood all to itself which the city fathers allowed to flourish in the name of good business and the protection of decent women who otherwise would be threatened by sex-starved, lusty, loathsome men.

The saloon and pool halls along the way were poorly lighted so that the grime was less noticeable, and every bartender kept a club close at hand. The women who frequented these dives kept rooms upstairs and used them off and on during the night. The dusty street itself was fouled with manure, and a few drunks slept in dark niches near the boardwalk.

On occasion gunfire might erupt in the street, or the silent knife find its mark in an alley, but this class of people was ignored for the most part, and a murder on Cherry Avenue was just another event that had happened before and would happen again.

The folks on the west side of the tracks firmly believed that anyone stupid enough to go onto Cherry Avenue after dark deserved all that he got.

So it became a kind of a balance. The politicians taking the graft in the name of protecting decent women, while at the same time keeping the barbaric lawlessness hidden under the covers of "What you don't know won't hurt you."

It was a place where the bullies and brutes mingled

with the sharpers and shiners, and with the hard-eyed women eager to fleece them all.

Of all the taverns on Cherry Avenue, Studs Murphy's Palace was the biggest and most popular, because Studs saw to it that the free lunch was something more than bread and cheese, and that the women who hung out there were the best on the row, and that fighting inside was absolutely prohibited.

Down the street on either side, scurvy half-breeds and obsolete buffalo hunters could puke on the floor or piss in the corner, could catch every venereal disease known, and could die or be paralyzed from poisoned alcohol, or slashed across the guts with a sharp bowie for no reazon at all. But not in Studs Murphy's Palace.

Studs Murphy maintained an elevated station, like a small stage, where he could watch over the whole bawling crowd with a two-bore ten-gauge shotgun said to be loaded with horseshoe nails and fishhooks in one charge, and rock salt in the other. If you still wanted to wreak havoc after the dose of salt, Studs was prepared to make an oozy corpse with the other.

The Palace was like a familiar home to Bull Basham. He'd spent most of his life under a fly-specked pressed-tin ceiling such as this one amidst the crowd noise and the wondrous costumes the sporters could concoct out of a few feathers and black net.

He saw the two bouncers who were just as big and unyielding as he was himself, and nodded to them, for they were all of the same physical fraternity and knew their business as well as any professional in any other field knew his.

Moving up to the bar, Bull automatically sized up the tall, yellow-haired bartender for signs of mean-ness, such as hitting you over the head with a bung starter when you weren't looking, then decided he'd have a shot of whiskey with a beer chaser.

Unsmiling, fast as forked lightning, the bartender put the two glasses on the bar and said, "Twenty cents."

After knocking down the shot, Bull Basham savored the beer, taking little sips like a swallow from a still pond as he considered how to gain some extra bonus out of the new business.

He reckoned they thought he was just a big mauler with his brains knocked out, and it pleased him to have them think so, but like most men, he was ambitious day and night, and he knew that somewhere in the scheme there was a crack where he could drive a wedge and break out a sizable purse from it.

Now, if he could find the girl, maybe he could use her for the wedge.

He ordered another shot and let his ideas percolate around in his loosened mind.

"Live around here?" he asked a scrawny old gaffer standing alongside him having a beer.

"I been around awhile," Skofer replied. "What do you want to know?"

"I'm lookin' for my niece. She's somewhere in town, but I lost her address. Name of Elizabeth . . ." Bull hesitated; he didn't know whether to say Greer or Veitengruber or Faraday, then he decided to straddle the fence.

"Elizabeth what?" the old man with the gray stubble on his sunken cheeks asked.

"Her maiden name was Faraday, but she married a guy name of Greer. So she could be goin' under either one."

"Faraday or Greer. Elizabeth." The old duffer took a sip of his beer and looked over his shoulder, then whispered, "I know most of the sporters on Cherry Avenue, but that name don't come to mind."

"She ain't a sporter," Bull growled.

"Don't get mad, friend," Skofer chuckled. "I've known a lot of sporters, and I wasn't ashamed to walk up Main Street with one on a Sunday morning. Why, one time up there in Miles City—"

"Oh, shut up," Bull said, turning his back on the old windbag, trying to think of another way of finding the girl besides asking every old soak on the street who wouldn't know anyway.

"The name Elizabeth Faraday is familiar in a way to me," a voice from behind said, and Bull turned around again to see a young, dark-faced man with oily black curls, moving around the old codger and coming close.

"How familiar would you say?" Bull murmured, his little eyes sizing up the dude in his fancy clothes. Some kind of a whoremaster, he assumed. Can't fight with his hands, so he'll have a little derringer inside that frock coat someplace.

"I'm sorry, I didn't get your name," the greasy dude said politely in a strange accent.

"Brown. Who are you?" Bull seized the dude by his lapels and drew him close so that no one could see the hold that effectively kept the dude's hand away from his hideout two-shooter.

The old man didn't move. He was talking to himself. . . . "Her name was Samantha or Lucretia—something like that—and when I come downstairs with her corset around my head, boy howdy, don't you think I got a cheer from the boys!"

Rene said quickly, "My name is Randy Armour, and I'm a personal friend of Studs Murphy."

Relaxing his grip, Bull Basham said, "Tell me all

about Elizabeth Faraday, my friend, and I'll buy the next round."

"What name was it? Elizabeth Hardesty? Yes, I know an Elizabeth Hardesty—in New Orleans."

"Don't give me that, mister," Bull growled. "You heard me right enough the first time."

Skofer chortled, ". . . then me'n that girl, we was goin' back to her room, and damned if I didn't fall through the partition and land right onstage! Had to do something with everybody laughing at me . . ."

"Shut up, old man!" Bull growled. "I can't hear."

"Nothing in life is ever free," Rene said with a warm, rosy-lipped smile.

"I'm her uncle. I want to talk to her about her dad," Bull said.

"Definitely not the same person." Rene smiled. "I'm sorry I bothered you."

He knows, Bull thought, but he's a sharper.

Under Studs Murphy's shotgun, Bull could hardly drag the smaller man outside. He had to put some kind of a deal together right then, or just go back to Sark and say, *he knows, you handle it.*

In that way he'd lose his leverage. No. He needed this oily little pimp, and the pimp knew it. Hard to make deals when you're in the blind, and if he failed somehow, Sark and Weed would be meaner than brass knuckles.

"All right, stranger," Bull said, appearing to give it up, "I'll just have to keep on lookin'."

". . . so I grabbed myself a chair from somebody in the band and started scootin' it around the stage like it was my horse, ayellin', 'Whoa, Red! Whoa, Red!' . . ."

"Shut up, I said!" Bull yelled.

". . . and that's how I got to be called Red!" Skofer grinned up at Bull, his washed-out blue eyes shining.

"Even though my hair was straight black in those days—"

"I wish you'd go talk to somebody else," Bull said, holding down his anger.

"No offense, mister." Skofer crowded in closer. "I recollect there was a Hardesty down in Texas, but we all just called her Butterbutt."

"Get outta here!" Bull roared, and Skofer backed off, carrying his half-full beer stein carefully.

"What's the trouble, boys?" One of the bouncers moved in smoothly.

"He was talking about names, and I was just telling him about how up in Miles City they changed my name from Blue to Red on account of I had a horse—"

"Fine," the bouncer said. "Go take a walk."

"He started it!" Skofer protested. "Wantin' to know the name of his niece. Why you pickin' on an old guy like me?"

The bouncer looked at Basham and decided he could handle him one way or another. The oily dude with him meant nothing except a hideout gun.

"You two better set at a table. This old gent has earned his spurs here."

The last thing in the world Bull wanted was to call attention to himself and his pigeon, and he quickly made up a broad grin and said, "Sure. The old gent's got a right to talk to himself all night if he can stand listening to himself."

Taking a grip on Rene's shoulder, Bull propelled him off into a dark corner to an empty table.

"Great John the Baptist," he whistled as he sat Rene down, "that old bastard nearly got us kicked out."

"He wasn't bothering me," Rene said mildly, his

olive-shaped brown eyes dreamy behind long black eyelashes.

"We'll make a deal," Bull Basham said, trying to be canny and wise at the same time. "I'll cut you in half of my share if you deliver the girl."

"My friend," Rene replied smoothly, "It's not so simple. I need to know if any harm can come to her. I need to know the details of your proposition."

"Not until I see the girl. Then I'll fill you in."

"You don't trust me?" Rene protested.

"There's eighty thousand dollars in it. We split it, fifty-fifty," Bull said, guessing a number, then doubling it.

"Would you care to advance me twenty percent of that right now?" Rene asked, deadly serious.

"When I see her," Bull lied.

"No, my friend. I'm wasting my time. Other people are looking for her too. If all you can do is talk, then we have nothing left to talk about."

Bull Basham's mind was locked in a paralysis. He could think of no way to get the advantage without giving away too much. He had to think it over.

Rene smiled knowingly. Whatever it turned out to be was all his.

"All right," Bull said heavily, "I've got a partner I've got to talk to. I'll meet you tomorrow."

"Fine. You must remember that the lady in question may be elsewhere. Possibly she cannot be produced at a moment's notice. Take your time."

"Here, tomorrow night. Same time," Bull growled, trying to think of some way to get the oily little bastard alone where he could just beat the pie waddin' out of him and then make his deal.

"I'll be leaving, Mr. Brown." Rene smiled, rose quickly, and was away through the crowd and out the doorway before Bull could even say, "Wait, I want to show you the alley."

As the doors closed, Bull looked around the crowded room and saw the old coot with the cocky, half-starved face waving at Bull to come on over and listen to a yarn.

Bull stomped out of the Palace pounding his fists together, trying to think.

6

The senator's home office was simple enough, paneled with golden oak and containing only two desks and a few chairs. The senator was able to make do with only one secretary, who kept the records in a beautiful and easily read Spencerian script, and the senator himself sat some hours every day at the larger desk, backed up by an American flag and the Kansas sunflower flag with the motto: *Ad Astra Per Aspera.*

Seated before him in a straight-backed chair, without portfolio or papers of any kind, Sam Benbow was doing his best, trying to reach the stars through difficulty, but failing.

"Senator, the National Trail would let the stockmen of this country bring cheap beef to all the poor people in the East."

"It's true, Mr. Benbow." The gray-headed, gray-mustached senator smiled easily. "There's no doubt about it. But your National Trail from the Red River to Canada would be six miles wide through the state of Kansas, a state whose interests I represent, not the poor people of the East."

"But the southern herds going north would bring along a lot of business opportunities for the Kansas people, and surely the federal government ought to think about donating a little land to the cattlemen after the millions of acres of public domain they've given the railroads."

"They should, but they won't, Mr. Benbow." The senator shook his head, his famous flowing gray hair moving like a mist in a breeze. "There are three obstacles, insurmountable in my opinion, to the idea of a National Trail from Texas to Montana. One is the Kansas Quarantine Laws, which must be enforced. Second is the Kansas farmer. Be he an Arkansas traveler or a Russian immigrant, he wants to farm. And three, the northern ranges are near to overcrowding already with Texas cattle, and the northerners are opposed to more longhorns eating their grass."

"But it's not their grass. It's the public's grass." Sam tried one last time, but knew that despite the genial manners of the old politician, he was not moving the National Trail forward by one stride of a longhorn steer.

"I'm very glad you stopped by, Sam. Always a pleasure to talk to you." The senator stood and shook Sam's hand, which signaled the conclusion of Sam's pitch.

Going down the broad steps of the Topeka Capitol Building, Sam made up his mind to quit or ask for a transfer to where there were real cattle.

He'd been hired at first by the South Texas Stockman's Association to catch a gang of shrewd and hard-fighting rustlers. He'd done that, and they'd asked him to stay on and help keep the old northern trail open.

But the senator was right. The Montana and Wyoming ranchers didn't want any more longhorn blood in their upgraded herds, which were bringing better prices per animal than the longhorn.

Money makes the mare go, he sighed, and I'm leaving this town as soon as I can get Missy Elizabeth Faraday's problem settled.

Once he made up his mind that he was finished as a lobbyist, Sam's spirits rose as if a draft of clean country air had entered his spirit and lifted the burden he'd been carrying around longer than he wanted to.

If he could whistle, he'd have been whistling. If he knew how to skip, he would have been skipping down the street. If he could have given a loud Coleman County *hooo-wheee* on the city street without starting a panic, he would have hollered at the top of his lungs, but as it was, he settled for a big, foolish smile on his battered face and a jaunty stride down the boardwalk.

Of course, he'd lost the battle, but it had been a hopeless dream from the start. The Texans were just going to have to change and breed up the longhorn to compete with the northern steers. It'd take some time, but they'd get to it all right on their own. Any time a Texican needed to lean on the federal government for help, Sam Benbow was ready to hang his head and ride for Mexico.

Stopping in at Sullivan's, Sam ordered oysters on the half shell and a stein of golden beer.

"Sometimes you're a hard man to find, Cap'n." Skofer's tone indicated a mild and self-righteous reproval, which meant to Sam that he'd discovered a dead cert way to beat chuck-a-luck, inherited a barrel of aged whiskey, or encountered a lovely young dancing girl looking for a mature professor to nurse along.

Sprinkling the platter of oysters with pepper sauce, Sam pretended not to hear him.

"I said, I've been looking for you," Skofer tried again. "We've got business."

"Haven't you heard, Skofer? I just resigned from the desk job and am moving over into the cattle business."

"Cattle business! By the Bard, Cap'n, what about Billy Faraday?"

"You can handle that easy enough," Sam said, chasing a tasty morsel with the good, malty beer. "Just go talk to Elizabeth, and sooner or later she'll remember some piece of information that'll lead you straight to Billy's grave."

"Sam Benbow, it's not like you to overdrink, especially before noon." Skofer shook his head sorrowfully. "Likely it's what I been afraid of, old John Barleycorn finally inserted his claws in your gizzard."

"Been dragged down some," Sam admitted, "but I'm on my way back up."

"Sam, I ran into your cousin George Brown late last night," Skofer said, looking off at an imaginary horizon. "He said you was a cut lower'n a rabid polecat with the clap."

Sam dropped the oyster off the shell, then quickly caught it in his glass of beer. Placing the stein back on the bar, he looked down at Skofer and growled, "Now, that's some unfinished business that interests me."

"Your hands are still fast enough." Skofer nodded at the oyster floating in the mug of beer. "I'm glad of that in case we have to shoot a few of these hombres down on Cherry Avenue."

"Cherry Avenue." Sam nodded.

"That's where I trapped him, Cap'n," Skofer said proudly.

"I'll see that you get a medal, Skofer." Sam downed his beer, oyster and all. "You sure it wasn't the other way around?"

"If it was him that dogged me, I doubt I'd be here trying to make a clear and responsible report to you, Cap'n," Skofer said stiffly.

"Report, Sergeant."

"He asked me if I knew an Elizabeth Greer or Faraday, couldn't seem to make it clear which it was, but he was looking for me to bite on one or the other, and I didn't. I entertained him awhile with some of my heroic exploits in Montana territory, but before I could quite finish, a slippery gypsy-looking sharper sidled up and started making as strange a palavering as I ever heard."

"So what did this oily gypsy have to say?"

"That's it. He said at first he might know her and then backed off and said, no, it's the wrong one. Then they went off and had a confab at a back table."

"That all?"

"Not exactly. I got the notion they were negotiating about sharing some money and they'd meet again tonight."

"So they're looking for Elizabeth, thinking she can put them on to some money, and her fiancé wants to sell her out."

"I'd surmise that to be correct."

"I'd surmise I'd like to crack their heads together," Sam growled.

"But first we ought to warn Miss Elizabeth."

"Warn her about what? Her sweetie? She's a big girl. She picked him, and she don't want to be proved wrong."

"Sam, it doesn't make a nevermind if she's a knotheaded female, she's Billy's daughter."

"Somethin' to that," Sam admitted, the euphoria of the hour before fading away as he came to grips with the problem of Billy.

... *Tell him I'd like him to make it right* ... the letter had said, just taking it for granted Sam would get to the bottom of the mess and deal out some justice.

"I reckon you're right, Skofer." Sam nodded. "We're goin' to do it even if she's too damned dumb to know beans from buckshot."

Tossing a quarter onto the bar, he led the way outside and on down the street to Ira's Lunch.

"Cap'n, you forgot to buy me a beer!" Skofer sputtered as he tried to keep up with Sam's long stride.

"I don't want you prey to old John Barleycorn's claws adraggin' you down."

"I'm on to him," Skofer protested. "I know just how far I can go with him!"

It being too late for breakfast and too early for the blue plate special, the restaurant was empty of customers. Even old Ira had pegged off somewhere, leaving Elizabeth in charge.

Skofer sat at the counter next to Sam and drummed on the counter nervously.

"What would you like, gentlemen?" Elizabeth asked without her usual warmth.

"Coffee for me, and beer for John Barleycorn's latest victim," Sam said.

She poured the coffee and found a bottle of beer in the cool box for Skofer, then asked, "Anything else?"

"We need to talk about your beau," Sam said.

"Rene Armenescu is my personal and private business," she retorted.

"Not if you're spilling our personal and private business into his big, greasy ears," Sam said stolidly.

"By heaven, Sam Benbow," she gasped, and took a

deep breath, biting her lips to keep from blessing Sam out in more explicit terms.

"Ma'am?" Sam asked mildly, "Have you told that sweet-smelling purty-posy feller anything?"

"Why?" she demanded sharply.

"Because my office and room have been searched, and if you're holding back somethin', you'll be next."

"What is so important?" she asked.

"Skofer just reminded me that Billy asked me to make it square, and I owe him, not you, that debt. He asked me to pay up in that letter, and that's what I aim to do, even if it means I turn your purty-posy upsides down and shake him some."

"Miss Elizabeth," Skofer put in before she could start blowing off steam, "that Rene feller isn't the type of man you think he is. You been off on a farm all your life."

"That's exactly what they said over there at Veitengruber," she fired back. "You're no different than they are!"

"Seems like you're one against the world," Sam said quietly. "Those Veitengrubers want you back."

"You people make it so hard!" she wailed. "You won't let a person live her own life, grow up, expand her living experiences, learn something of the world! No, you've got to shut out anything or anybody unusual that comes along."

"Why would we do that?" Sam asked pointedly.

"You're fired!" she cried out. "I don't need your help anymore. My daddy picked all the wrong people. I know he meant well, but he sure set me down in the middle of a briar patch!"

Putting her hands to her face, she ran weeping into the kitchen, where Sam could hear Melba Armsbury talking soothing nonsense to her.

Sam laid down a silver quarter and said, "Best we

83

move out before she throws scaldin' water on us both."

"That man sure has her hornswiggled," Skofer said sadly as they left the restaurant. "You think she told him?"

"Sure she did. But she's holding back something. It's a question now if she's already given it to posy boy or not."

"I don't get your meanin', Cap'n."

"I been thinkin' there should have been an envelope holding those two letters and the gold piece."

"Then where is it?"

"She said she burned it without thinking on it bein' important."

"But she didn't."

"My feelin's exactly."

"Then as soon as the gypsy sells her to Cousin George, George is going to find that envelope."

"You are just as bright as new money today, Skofe. Now, what do you think you ought to do about it?"

Skofer closed his rheumy eyes a moment, then abruptly opened his mouth and said, "No, I can't."

"Skofe, you got to."

"No. You're the one owes Billy, not me!"

"Seems I recollect Billy packin' you in over his saddle one time."

"That's because I was drinking in that Charlottesville tavern."

"And the Yankees was comin' in the front door as Billy was draggin' you out the back. How long you think you'd have lasted as a prisoner of war?"

"Don't say no more, Cap'n. I'm surrendering right now." Skofer threw up his hands in defeat. "How do I do it?"

"There's a back door to the restaurant. I'll keep 'em busy in the front."

"When?"

"I can't think of a better time than right now," Sam said cheerfully. "Just go down the alley and try the second door on the left."

"Oh, Cap'n, the things you get me into," Skofer quavered, walking down the alley out of sight.

Sam turned back and arrived at the door of the restaurant at the same time as old Ira came along, pegging heavily from the other direction.

"Howdy, Sam," Ira boomed. "Hear about the carpenter was buildin' a house and was throwin' half the nails away?"

"No, I reckon not," Sam said, following Ira into the restaurant.

"'How come you're throwin' them nails away?' a feller asks this carpenter. 'Why, can't you see?' the carpenter said. 'The heads are on the wrong end.' 'Why, you mulehead,' the feller says, 'them nails are all right, they're just for the other side of the house!'"

Sam laughed politely as Ira pegged back behind the counter and asked, "Coffee?"

"And a piece of apple pie, please, if there's anybody workin' in the kitchen."

"Coffee and pie," Ira yelled. "Man likely to cry!"

When Elizabeth appeared with the wedge of apple pie and a mug of coffee from the kitchen, she nearly dropped the pie and slopped the coffee. Her tearstained face revealed the shock of their just-finished encounter, and she wasn't ready for any more.

"What's got your goat, girl?" Ira demanded.

"Just the usual," she said.

Used to the vagaries of womenfolks, Ira was satisfied with that.

Sam said calmly, "Don't worry, ma'am, everything is for the best."

"Every cloud has a silver lining," she responded.

"And if you spit up in the air, you'll get it in the face!" Ira laughed jovially.

"And it'll all come out in the wash. . . ." She smiled ruefully, dabbed at her eyes, and then glared at Sam. "You can be quite upsetting at times."

"It's the nature of us untamed broncos," Sam said. "All we know is popping brush and buckin' like hell."

"You mean you can't waltz?" she asked, teasing.

"I'm more of a stomper and a screamer myself." Sam smiled.

"I've been learning a little," she said without thinking. "Rene—" she caught herself, and Sam finished it for her.

"Has been showin' you a few steps?"

She nodded, not sure whether to be mad, glad, or sad.

"I suppose it's mighty uplifting in many ways." Sam nodded agreeably. "Likely he's got some plans for your future on the stage."

"He's mentioned a career, but I'll need some lessons and new clothes. . . ."

"Goin' to have to kill that sucker," Sam murmured to himself, his eyes glazing over with a red fury.

"Sam Benbow!" she yelled. "You promised you'd be nice!"

Seeing Skofer leaning into the doorway, Sam said crisply, "Much obliged for your time, ma'am."

"Sam, don't you touch that man!" she said hotly.

"I ain't gonna touch him. I'm goin' to shoot him so much, he's goin' to bleed perfume." Sam grinned.

Putting a dime and a nickel on the counter, he tipped his hat, walked out to the boardwalk, and taking the small man's shoulder, guided him on down the street.

"Get it?"

"Got it, Cap'n, but I sure was sweating blood, fingering through her valise."

"It's all for a worthy cause," Sam said loftily, "and you'll get your reward in heaven."

"Suppose I could have a cool beer before we go much farther towards those pearly gates?" Skofer wheezed.

"I'll buy," Sam said, letting Skofer lead the way into the tavern.

"Reckon we can use the back room?" Sam asked Sullivan.

"You goin' to learn singin' from Skofer?" Sullivan grinned.

"He's gone past that stage," Sam said. "He's ready to teach old Rip how to drink beer with his eyes shut."

"If Skofe can do it," Sullivan said, "Rip can, too."

"You two are goin' to get tonsilitis hazing your betters," Skofer retorted hotly. "Say one thing, I don't put oysters in my beer and then guzzle them down alive and wiggling."

Amidst the hoots and laughter of his two persecutors, Skofer stalked off into the back room.

"Reckon I better be more careful," Sam said over his shoulder. "Teasin' the camp cook is about as risky as brandin' a mule's butt."

Pacing the floor nervously, Skofer appeared to be agonizing over his act of burglary. "Never again, Sam. Don't never send me into a woman's boudoir one time more, because I won't do it."

"We had to do it, Skofe, for her own good. Understand?"

"I don't believe she'd take it that way."

"Likely not," Sam sighed. "Can you part with it for a minute or two?"

"Honest, Sam, I had to dig around through unmentionables I don't even know the name of," Skofer said. "I'd as soon pet a corpse."

"The loot," Sam said patiently.

Handing over the worn envelope, Skofe muttered, "I don't know what my mama would say about me now. . . ."

"Miss Elizabeth Faraday, Veitengruber, Missouri. That's her, all right. Now, the postmark says Arboreal Splendor, Kansas. Ever hear of it?"

"Out west of Junction City someplace." Skofer nodded. "Nothing much there after the land promoters left."

"And the return address is Mrs. Ruby O'Banion, Sylvan Grove, Kansas. Know that one?"

"I'd guess it'd be smaller'n Arboreal Splendor and on upriver."

"What would be the nearest train stop?"

"Ellsworth likely, or Fort Hays, but they'd be a ways south."

"Can't leave Elizabeth here on her own, not whilst her sweetie is trying to sell her off," Sam said, shaking his head.

"Why do you suppose she held that envelope out on you?" Skofer asked.

"Scared. She can read as well as we can, and it don't take overmuch furniture in the upstairs parlor to figure there's a considerable number of brand-new gold pieces out there in Sylvan Grove."

"How do you figure?"

"He puts a new gold piece on the message that says this ain't the first or the last. I guess that's plain as a bear turd in the fryin' pan."

Reluctantly, Bull Basham opened his eyes to the noonday sun. It took him a minute to remember where he was, but when he saw through the haze that enveloped his throbbing head a short, squat lady drawing a black net stocking up over her ankle, up the sturdy calf to the dimpled knee, then tugging it on up over the heavy, fleshy thigh rippling with fat, he remembered.

Her cheeks were sagging with folds of flesh, and her eyes looked like dried prunes.

"Who the hell are you?" he groaned.

"My name's Penny," she recited automatically. "I can be bright or bad, however you like it."

"Where's my wallet?" he growled suspiciously, sitting up.

"Where you left it, mister," she retorted wearily.

Bull poked his hand down into his boot and found his wallet. There was still money left in it.

"Don't worry, mister, I earned my dollar and you left no tip," she said angrily.

"Shut up. I don't want to hear your jawin'."

Slipping on a pair of orange leather high-buttoned shoes, she finished dressing, stood, and asked hostilely, "What are you waitin' on?"

"I'm waitin' for you to get your big butt out of here." Bull made a fist and cocked his elbow.

"Okay, honey," she said neutrally. "Any time you want to have a party, just ask for Penny, bright or bad, however you like it."

She went out the door and down the hall, while Bull Basham cursed himself for getting liquored up the night before. He vaguely remembered fighting somebody in the alley, knocking him down, then giving him the boot.

Later he'd met the old whore and bought her a couple of drinks. She'd looked a hell of a lot better then.

Before that, floating up in his memory, was the oily

pimp with the black, curly hair. He'd slipped away. Bull had tried to follow him, but lost him almost immediately. Slick as a water snake, that dude, he thought. Why didn't I just quit for the day and go to bed?

He padded over to the washstand and put the pitcher to his mouth, rinsed the thick crust free, and spit it all out onto the floor.

Better. Damn, should have asked the old nautch if she knew the slippery whoremaster. What good would it do? Sure, she knows him, but she don't know him well enough to know the girl too.

Question was, should he tell banker Sark about him or not?

Sark knew what he was doing.

The pimp was too smart to produce the girl without some sort of a safety, some guarantee that he'd be paid.

If he got nervous, he'd run. Lose him, you got nothin'. Give him to Sark, you still got a chance of winning something.

Getting into his wrinkled checkered suit, he didn't bother to wash his face or shave.

He wanted a beer to get him started, then he could think up some way to get the pimp back in an alley where he could beat his pretty face to a dime's worth of dogmeat, and get the truth out of him.

Coming down the wooden steps of the Cherry Avenue rooming house, he went down the boardwalk a few doors to Murphy's Palace, where he downed the first glass of beer, then nipped at the next one as he considered his moves. Jab, jab, jab with the left, then come across with the right. Stick him with that left until he's cross-eyed, then the overhand right on the jaw. The winner and new champion, Bull Basham!

No more of those old dollar-a-night dock wallopers.

No more of this green beer. No more blue plate specials. No more cheap suits that looked like worn-out horse blankets before they were a week old. No more taking insults. No more of Weed's spittin' next to his boot.

Call me Mister. Mr. Bullard Basham, esquire.

Bring in Sark and Weed, or not?

He couldn't decide. Greed was balanced against survival, and left him on dead center.

Goddammit, his throbbing head agonized, if I could just find that whoremonger, I'd sure smack the pretty smile right off his face.

I can't do it, he thought. I ain't smart enough.

Defeated by himself, he dropped a dime on the bar and, like a humble servant, trudged down the street, crossed the tracks, and entered the First Charter Bank of Kansas.

7

In Murphy's Palace—heavy with the smell of semi-annually changed long johns exuding sweat and occasional small voidings, bitter with eye-watering cigar smoke, raucous with coarse laughter—the atmosphere was meaner'n a bagful of rattlesnakes as lonely men drank to recover some hope from the day's hopelessness, sensitive to any sign of insult, ready to flare up and fight over a hard look or loose word. Yet all were held in check by the presiding eminence, Studs Murphy himself on his podium.

In one corner banker Sark, the lean and lethal weed, and Bull Basham sat at a table obscured in shadows. Basham had a glass of whiskey in front of him, and the banker was sipping Spanish brandy.

In the opposite corner, equally obscured in the dim lamplight, Skofer and Sam watched and waited, tasting the green beer once in a while to relieve the tension.

"Where's posy-face?" Sam grumbled. "It's gettin' past my beddy-bye time."

"If I was him and knew my way around this hurdy-gurdy, I'd be up there in the dark hall that probably leads back to the cribs," Skofer murmured, watching the dark upstairs corridor out of the corner of his eyes.

"Is there a back stairway?"

"Bound to be." Skofer nodded.

"So he sneaks up there from the alley. Might even have a sporter up there working for him. He sees you and me, he sees Cousin George and Elijah Sark, then decides there's too much against him and he'll work out some other scheme. Some way to get to Sark without us ridin' herd on him."

"That's how I would read it," Skofer muttered. "It'd been better if I'd played the drunk at the bar, and left you outside."

"It's not too late," Sam said quickly. "Go ahead, old pard, play the part you know so well."

"Sam, I'd rather climb up a tree full of tigers," Skofer protested weakly.

"Sorry, we're out of tigers this week." Sam smiled and went out the batwing doors, looking neither left nor right.

Avoiding horsemen and buckboards, he made his way across the street where he could be ready for action.

Skofer took his empty glass to the bar, his head wobbling, his step timid.

"Gimme another, bar-dog," he croaked, and flashed a crazy smile.

The bartender refilled the beer stein, took Skofer's nickel, and moved on down the bar.

Skofer thought he should have asked Sam what he was supposed to do if the scented whoremonger came down the stairway and went over to Sark's table.

For sure Armenescu mustn't give away the identity of Elizabeth or where she stayed.

Tapping his glass on the bar lightly in two-four time, he commenced to sing an old party song to himself.

> "Old Joe Clark, the preacher's son,
> He preached all over the plain.
> The highest text he ever took
> Was high low Jack and the game . . ."

Gradually his sense of elfin merriment took over from his confused worrying, and his voice grew louder and brought smiles to the faces of the men closest to him.

> "If you see that girl of mine,
> Tell her if you can,
> Wherever she goes to roll that dough,
> To wash her dirty hands . . ."

Someone nearby picked up on the chorus and joined in with Skofer, attracting more and more bystanders.

> "Round and round, Old Joe Clark,
> Round and around, we're gone.
> Round and around, Old Joe Clark,
> And bye bye Lucy Long . . ."

In some strange way, Skofer brought the attention of the raucous, unholy bunch of derelicts around to the song, their spirits lifting, their eyes shining, as they remembered the lyrics from better days.

"I wish I was in Arkansas,
  Settin' on a rail,
  Sweet potato in my hand
  And a possum by the tail . . ."

Gradually Skofer yielded the song over to the man standing behind him who had a big, strong voice.

"Old Joe Clark had a house.
  It was sixteen stories high.
  And every room in that big house
  Just smelled like chicken pie . . ."

Glancing up, Skofer saw that even old Murphy was stamping his feet and joining in on the choruses.

"I went down to Old Joe's house.
  He was eatin' supper.
  Stubbed my toe on the table leg
  And rammed my nose in the butter . . ."

He slowly backed away from the center of the songsters, giving the lead to the big, weathered man who probably had left the farm to work on a railroad before ending up here, and then slowly eased out of the circle, clapping his hands and singing away, but disappearing at the same time.

Out of the corner of his eye he saw a figure in striped pants and pale blue frock coat gliding down the stairway, unnoticed by anyone in the room.

Quickly the figure disappeared in the shadows, but Skofer had seen the black, shiny ringlets coiffed around the dark, oily face.

Turning, he spread out his arms and charged the swift Armenescu as he crossed toward Sark's table.

Armenescu dodged aside adroitly, then sensing a

trap, turned back and ran for the stairway while Skofer bounced out the front door yelling, "Sam! Sam!"

Sam came bursting in like a bull from the chute, but Armenescu had already disappeared down the dark upstairs hall.

As Skofer yelled, "Around back!" a big, looping right hand caught Sam in the back of the neck, snapping his head back and sending him sliding face downward on the sawdust floor.

As Bull Basham rushed forward, ready to slam his boot into Sam's ribs, Skofer suddenly appeared like a small, feisty terrier, driving Basham off course with his shoulder.

Basham hit the old man on the side of the head with a quick, short right hook that dropped Skofer like a handful of small change.

Sam took that moment to roll aside and get to his feet, still dizzy from the sucker punch, but fully aware he was in for a fight.

Basham charged forward before Sam could get set, and drove a left hook into Sam's midriff, then brought up a powerful right uppercut that grazed Sam's chin.

As Sam fell back, Murphy stood in his podium and yelled, "That's enough!" and fired a load of rocksalt next to Basham's boot.

The two bouncers arrived, and Basham said, "I'll go easy. Just make sure that fancy cowboy comes along."

The two bouncers dragged the groggy Sam to the door, pitched him out onto the boardwalk, and went back in after Skofer.

Bull Basham watched his victim crawling towards the hitch rail, using it to pull himself up.

Grinning with pleasure, he took three quick strides toward Sam, meaning to cave in Sam's ribs with his boot. At the last moment Sam fell to one side so that

Basham's boot collided with the hitch rail, and at the same time, Sam's boot kicked the left ankle out from under Basham's bulk, sending the big man into the street.

Gaining a second to clear his head, Sam climbed to his feet and stood tottering as the pair were ringed by blood-crazed bystanders, lusting for someone else's pain.

"Give him the boot!"

"Tear him to pieces!"

"Jab his eyes!"

As Bull got to his feet, Sam stepped forward and unleashed a thunderbolt right hand to Basham's jaw, a blow that would normally coldcock a steer. Basham blinked, then suddenly came up from a crouch with a vicious left to Sam's jaw. Sam hardly had time to turn his head before he saw it coming, and the elbow that followed it cracked him across the cheekbone and sent him staggering back into the crowd.

Hands pushed him forward into the ring, and Sam was aware now of the power of his opponent, who knew all the tricks of street fighting and also had the kick of a mule's hind leg in each fist.

Knowing he couldn't take much more of such heavy pounding, he commenced to dodge and duck, getting his brain clear, his coordination back, his reaction time down to near zero.

"Get in and fight, you yellow belly!" a scrawny derelict cried out manfully, and shoved Sam forward into a hard right to the belt buckle.

"Sock him one, cowboy, right twixt his legs," old Penny, bright or bad, yelled gleefully.

Basham was breathing heavily now as the earlier adrenaline faded away and his poor conditioning caught up with him.

Sam came in, bobbing and weaving, throwing light

punches that peppered the big Basham, making him forget Sam's power, and just as he felt a light tap, tap on his chin from Sam's left, he forgot his shoulder was low, and Sam's right hand, like an anvil, crossed over and smashed the angle of his jaw below the ear.

The blow sent Bull to his knees, but instead of following it up with a knee to the face or a boot to the gut, Sam stepped back and gave Basham time to get to his feet, then he moved in swiftly and hooked him in the belly twice, bringing down his guard again, then crossing the massive right over to the same point as before.

Again Sam stepped back and waited as the big man fell, but this time Basham, instead of climbing to his feet, dove at Sam's knees, tripping Sam into the dirt. In a moment he was trapped in Basham's huge arms.

Basham, kneeling over Sam, threw a right hand at his face, but Sam whipped his head aside as the fist came down, then arched his back, reversed the angle of his spine, and brought the crown of his head flat against Basham's scarred eyebrows, inflicting two bleeding gashes over Basham's eyes.

Basham pawed at his bleeding face, and Sam threw him aside in a quick lunge and got to his feet.

His chest heaving, he watched the mauler for any more sudden tricks, but Basham was pacified, for the moment at least.

Skofer was sitting on the boardwalk with his back to the saloon wall, his eyes closed.

"Hey, Skofe, you in there?" Sam asked, bending down.

"I'm all right, Sam," Skofer said miserably. "I just couldn't bear to watch him beat you like that."

"Wasn't all that bad," Sam said, touching the swelling lumps and welts on his face.

"How'd you beat him?" Skofer asked, looking up.
"Used my head." Sam smiled.

Rene Armenescu knew his ground as a weasel knows his range, and using the cover of dilapidated buildings and parked wagons, he made his way rapidly to the tracks, then, pausing by a boxcar, listened for signs of pursuit.

He heard a ruckus going on over on Cherry Avenue, but that wasn't unusual.

Straightening his coat, he walked down Topeka Avenue, still keeping to the shadows, but not as a ferret or criminal, only as a man who might be out for his evening stroll.

With his meeting spoiled by the loony old drunk, he knew he had to act quickly in case Elijah Sark had seen his face. He'd recognized the banker off in the corner with the big bruiser and another man, and realized then just how high the stakes were.

Coming into the empty restaurant, he found Elizabeth hanging up her apron.

"I'm glad I'm in time," Armenescu said with an urgency in his voice.

"I was just leaving."

"We've got to hurry and find a safe place for you," Armenescu warned her, improvising a new scheme.

"Safe?" I couldn't be any safer than I am right here," she laughed.

"Listen, Elizabeth, I saw three of those Veitengrubers having a drink down at Sullivan's. They're looking for you."

"Whatever for?" she asked, feeling a sense of panic at the very sound of the name. "I'm finished with them."

"They claim you stole their savings that they'd hidden under a rock in the hearth."

"I wouldn't ever do such a thing!"

"I know that, but they say they discovered the money gone right after you ran off, and you'll either pay it back or go to jail."

"They're dead wrong!"

"Can you prove it?"

"I don't have to prove my innocence," she protested.

"That sounds fine for a politician's speech on the Fourth of July, but we've got to be practical. If you can hide out for a couple days, they'll have to go on back to the farm."

The story was credible enough; it would be just like them to blame her for anything that went wrong, because they hated her so much.

"I don't want to run off," she said. "Then they'll be sure I'm guilty."

"I know an out-of-the-way rooming house. It's pretty run-down, but it won't hurt for you to stay the night there. Meantime, I'll have a talk with them and get it straightened out."

"I'm scared to death of those people," she admitted. "If they ever got a hold of me, I'd rather die right now."

"We'd better hurry and talk later."

"Good night, Melba, good night, Ira!" she called back into the kitchen, and hearing their replies, closed the front door behind her.

Armenescu took her arm and guided her around to her room for her valise, then on down a side street toward the tracks.

In the darkness, Armenescu was smiling as he saw the first piece of his plan falling into place.

In Sullivan's washroom, Sam bathed the bumps and abrasions on his face, knocked the dust off his clothes and slouch hat, then, feeling better, returned to the bar, where Skofer was downing a glass of beer.

"Did you get a look at Armenescu?" Sam asked.

"Enough. He's slippery as peeled elm bark."

"I'm glad we spoiled their game, for a while at least."

"You know that gunfighter with Sark?" Skofer asked.

"Saw him once down in Laredo. Calls himself Loco Weed. He's fast as a cut cat, and he don't much care who he shoots either."

"Think you could beat him, Cap'n?" Skofer asked, tipping up his glass again.

"Hell, no. He's got nothin' to do all day but play with that six-gun while honest men are out punchin' cows for a livin'."

"I was afraid you'd say something like that," Skofer grumbled. "I guess I better get out my old Walker Colt and start practicing."

"You think you could lift it now that you're in your declining years, Skofe?" Sam grinned. "That old .44 weighs five pounds loaded."

"It's true she's a heavy brute, but she shoots straight and throws a half-ounce ball from here to yonder."

Sam felt a tugging at his coat sleeve and looked down at a freckle-faced boy with serious blue eyes.

"You Mr. Benbow? Sam Benbow?"

"That's me."

"Telegram for you, Mr. Benbow." The boy handed over a yellow sheet of paper folded twice.

Sam gave him a coin, and unfolded the paper and read,

INVESTIGATE BLOCK DIAMOND HERD RUSTLED NEAR MELVERN. STOCKMAN'S ASSOCIATION.

"Bad news?" Skofer asked, craning his neck high enough to read the message.

"No, but it's work to do. Where's Melvern?"

"About thirty miles south."

"Get the horses, boots, and saddles!" Sam said with pleasure.

"Won't it wait till I finish my beer?" Skofer complained.

"I'll get my guns and meet you at the livery stable."

Rene Armenescu watched the two riders, one dressed in Levi's, flannel shirt, and leather vest, big and easy in the saddle, the other hardly bigger than a jockey who rode with his stirrups so long that his scrawny butt was bouncing on the cantle of his saddle as they rode out of the livery and headed south.

Again he smiled as he saw the second piece of his plan fall into place.

Benbow and his partner should arrive down around Melvern long after sunrise, then they'd waste a couple hours trying to find some sign of the Block Diamond herd, and then they'd have a long ride back.

By then, he should be in the driver's seat and long gone on the morning train.

Moving on down the boardwalk, he came to a pair of heavy oak-paneled doors bearing a sign in gold leaf: *The Railroad Club.*

Armenescu paused to run his fingers through his black ringlets and straighten up his lapels, then opened the forbidding door and stepped inside onto a polished parquet floor. The bar across the room was small, with most of the room devoted to tables and chairs with padded seats. In the gloom he could see the elegant drapes that covered private cubicles, and though he knew he didn't belong here, he also figured that it wouldn't be long before these high-toned businessmen would welcome him.

There were no whores nor music, only the businessmen in conservative, expensive suits, making deals with one another, and other types of transactions with the politicians in the capital.

There's none of 'em any better than me, he thought, looking around at the hushed tables until a waiter in a red coat asked stiffly, "Something?"

"Is Mr. Sark here? My name is Rene Armenescu."

"I'll see." The waiter's hooded eyes flickered, and he retreated, slipped through a draped portal, reappeared after a moment and waved his hand at Rene.

"In here," he said shortly, disapproval written all over his face, and left Rene to poke his way through the heavy drapery into a small room that held a large round table and several chairs.

A hanging Rochester lamp revealed Elijah Sark, Weed, and Bull Basham finishing up their evening meal.

A black waiter in a red coat loaded up a tray with their dirty dishes and soundlessly left by a side door.

"Evening," Sark said without rising. "You know Weed and Bull?"

"We're acquainted," Armenescu said carefully. He hadn't expected the pug and the hardcase to be here in this posh place, but decided it would make his dealings faster and safer.

"Sit down," Sark said curtly. "We've been expecting you."

"How could—"

"You've got something to sell. It's perishable and you have to sell it in a hurry before it's worthless to us. Isn't that right?"

"I'm in no hurry," Armenescu said, lazily sitting

down and lighting a long, thin cigar. "I have all the time in the world."

"Fine. Then we'll see you next week," Sark said, an egg-sucking smile cracking his pouched lips.

"You underestimate me, Mr. Sark." Armenescu poured himself a small beaker of the Spanish brandy from a cut-glass carafe.

"What have you got to sell?" Sark came back with a sneer.

"I have Sam Benbow and I have the girl."

"What do you mean?" Sark's eyes hardened.

"You need her to find your treasure, and you have to get clear of Sam Benbow before he kills all of you."

"You got a big mouth for such a little tinhorn," Weed said.

"Save your insults, please. We all need each other. If any of these men are not full partners in your project, Mr. Sark, I suggest you dismiss them."

"Get out of here, Basham," the banker said, not taking his eyes off the sloe-eyed, olive-skinned Armenescu.

"Just a damned minute," Bull protested. "I earned some right tonight—"

"You're goin' to earn somethin' else, too, you don't mind," Weed said harshly. "Get out. I want to hear what the tinhorn has to say."

Grumbling, Bull rose and left by the side door.

"You're a full partner, Mr. Weed?" Armenescu asked softly, surprised.

"He is," Sark said. "Now, where's the girl?"

"I need a guarantee that I have a third share in the plunder, Mr. Sark."

"Just for the girl?"

"No, for getting Benbow off your trail, too, and whatever else is needed to secure the gold."

"What gold?" Sark's jaw clamped down hard.

"I know almost all of it, Mr. Sark; I only don't know where it is, but I can persuade the girl to tell me that."

"All right, there's some gold coin," Sark admitted. "How much?"

"Forty-six thousand dollars in twenty-dollar gold pieces."

"That's a lot of gold to carry around," Armenescu sighed.

"About a hundred and fifty pounds," Weed said.

"And you want a third of it for just one night's work." Sark shook his porky head.

"I'm sure it won't be that simple, Mr. Sark."

"If you knew what Weed and I have gone through because of that gold, you wouldn't be so easy about it," Sark growled.

"The girl's father was a partner?"

"More or less," Weed said.

"But you became separated."

"That son of a bitch was weasel-smart, like you," Weed snarled.

"I need a guarantee, Mr. Sark." Armenescu came back to the beginning. "I don't bluff, and I don't scare."

"No doubt you got it all figured out." The banker frowned.

"My notion is you would use me and the girl up until the money was in your hands, and then dispose of us."

"If I was you, I'd figure on somethin' like that," Weed said.

"I suggest that I write all of this down in a letter to the U.S. marshal. I suggest we all sign it, and I will leave it with a friend to mail in case I don't return by a certain date," Armenescu suggested easily, drawing on his cigar and letting the smoke trickle away from his lips.

"You're crazy," said Sark. "I'll sign nothing."

"When we return from our successful trip, I would, of course, return the document to you."

"Suppose you get snakebit?"

"It would be to your best interests to see that nothing like that happened to me."

"What about Benbow?" Sark asked.

"You have to kill him sooner or later. I'll tell you when and how to do it."

"When do we leave?" Weed asked.

"We'll take the westbound train first thing in the morning."

"How do you know it's west?" Weed demanded hotly.

"Because someone killed the lady's father before he could find where the old man had hidden the gold. You come from Ellsworth. You don't seem to be worried about any other person seeking the gold. I suggest that you were the ones who killed Bill Faraday."

"Why, you rotten—" Weed drew as he stood and stabbed the barrel of his Colt against Armenescu's pale forehead, an expression of wild fury on his thin face.

"Don't do it," snapped Sark. "He's right and you know it. You went too fast with Faraday, and you're close to making the same mistake twice."

Taking a deep breath, and letting it out slowly, the tall gunfighter stepped back and gently lowered the hammer down on a loaded chamber.

"Good thinking, Mr. Sark." Armenescu had a slight quaver in his voice, beads of sweat popping out on his smooth forehead. "Will you ask the waiter to bring us paper and pen and ink, please?"

8

Mrs. O'Banion in the past few days had climbed up into the small attic and crawled through the spiderwebs and fine dust, looking for a bag of gold. It wasn't there. Nothing was up there because nobody had ever gotten into the crawl space since the little house was nailed together.

Once she was certain the attic hadn't been tampered with or used as a hideout, she started with Billy's bedroom, examined the walls, and tapped the plaster, especially around the closet, where someone sure enough in the past had sawed out a board in the floor and made a storage place. But it held only a half jug of clear whiskey, and she could pretty well figure that her second husband, Henry O'Banion, had created that space to fool her when he wanted a drink. There was no sign of a gold piece in it anyway.

She went around the parlor in the same way, looking under the carpets, examining the rocks in the fireplace hearth, but once again she came up empty-handed.

She was persistent and thorough, but after searching the kitchen, she had to admit that it wasn't in the house.

Taking a lantern down into the storm cellar, she probed the dirt floor and walls with an iron bar, but the earth was hard and dry, and all she discovered were two bats who knifed through the shadows, scaring her half out of her wits when they touched her red hair.

Of course, the people of Sylvan Grove were aware that she was spending a lot of time in the little house, commenting on the street corners and over back fences as to when she'd gone to the house and when she left it, what she'd carried in or carried out, their small-town espionage system more effective than that of warring nations.

Still, being a veteran of that system, Ruby O'Banion was able to confuse its intelligence by carrying brooms and mops, buckets and baskets, back and forth between her own little house and the empty rental, which partly assured the neighbors that she was cleaning the place from top to bottom.

She took her broom to the whitewashed outhouse, with its simple single-wall construction, and quickly decided there was no bag of gold in there. Just to make sure, she poked her head down the hole and checked the area below the seat, but she knew Billy well enough to realize he wouldn't be that crude. The sack of lime in the corner was only a sack of lime. The dusty pile of newspapers and *Harper's Monthly*s were simply old paper. The outhouse was only an outhouse.

Next was the woodshed, where she unstacked and restacked a cord of cottonwood and ash billets for nothing.

I might as well be looking for the bluebird of happiness, she smiled at herself, and after futilely searching through the tool shed, moving old halters and hames, dried-out tar buckets and a broken wagon jack, she concluded the gold might just as likely be in a bank over at Ellsworth or buried out on the prairie. For sure it wouldn't be in the chicken house nor the adjacent workshop, but she had to look.

Using the brass key that hung on the wall by the back door, she unlocked the padlock, which fitted into a heavy wrought-iron hasp that Billy had forged and made himself.

Several times he'd told her he didn't want her to disturb the shop because he was the only one who understood his experimental project.

She had asked, "What kind of project?"

"It's an improvement on the steam engine using refined petroleum and alcohol." He'd tried to explain, but she didn't understand the principle of expanding water vapor, let alone the energy in his refined fuels.

Going on inside, she saw in the dim light the two oak barrels at the back of the shop where Billy stored the cracked corn and oats for his pet barred Rock hens and the mighty red-combed rooster with the angry black eyes, always strutting around and being foolish.

Looking around in the dim light that came from a single pane of glass in the wall, she saw Billy's small forge with foot-powered bellows, neat piles of iron bars, and copper ingots from which he'd made fancy hinges and iron locks in his spare time. On a rough plank bench that ran the width of the building was a variety of homemade projects Billy had worked on to pass the time. One was the miniature steam engine that he had tried to improve by adding things to the water. There were jugs of alcohol, and a box of gunpowder, as well as jars full of various kinds of acid.

Nearby was a glass demijohn marked "coal oil," and next to it was a tall, narrow copper pot with a bulging top from which came a coil of copper tubing that ran off to a gallon jug nearly full of an oily liquid. She recognized it as a still, but it was a different sort from those the whiskey makers used. He'd said something about the coal oil being too heavy to mix with the water in his steam engine, and he was working at making the coal oil into a richer, cleaner product, but she'd not paid it much attention.

He'd kept the shed locked because he was afraid some inquisitive boys might get hurt.

My, he was a handy man even though he only had the one good hand to work with, she thought. If he'd had a few more years, he just might have invented a whole new kind of steam engine.

The place smelled of oil and iron and ashes.

What could she do with the strange tools and devices he'd assembled? He was the only one who knew what they were for, and even if he'd learned something from his experiments, he'd never had a chance to finish up his project, and all was lost.

Everything looked to be so simple and wide open, there wasn't much use in poking around, looking for bags of gold.

Best she get busy and start cleaning out the chicken house.

After that, every morning she went over to Billy's house, unlocked the workshop, took a wooden scoop of cracked corn out of the feed barrel and tossed it into the chicken pen, gathered half a dozen brown eggs, then went back to her own little house and commenced washing someone else's dirty clothes on a scrub board propped in a copper boiler half-full of water and lye soap suds.

Far to the east of Sylvan Grove, down a lane guarded on both sides by locust pole fences with chalk rock posts, the two men rode along steadily in the moonlight, occasionally putting their horses into an easy lope, then drawing them down to a fast walk when their breathing became hoarse and short.

The road ran straight south and was well traveled during the day, but seldom at night.

"This was just prairie a year ago," Skofer grumbled whenever his horse shied away from a fence. "Them grangers are coming in so fast, they'll be out to Colorado in a couple more years. Four families on every square mile of the Big Pasture."

"It don't make sense," Sam said after they'd been riding an hour and the country remained fully settled and fenced. "There can't be any sizable herd of Texas cattle around here."

Every quarter of a mile they passed a dark farmhouse, and an occasional watchdog would run out to bark at them. Later on they saw lamps being lighted, and men carrying lanterns to their barns, starting their long day in darkness, and no doubt working in their fields until sundown or later.

"Spooks me," Sam said. "I reckon we're on a wild-goose chase."

The rosy dawn disclosed a bucolic paradise of little houses, big barns, fields of corn, and fenced pastures full of fat cattle.

At a crossroad, they saw a general store with a frame house alongside.

A hand-painted sign on the front of the store said Mercantile.

An old man wearing a shawl over his shoulders was padding from the house toward the store in felt slippers, still half-asleep.

"Mister," Sam called. "Say there, mister, how far to Melvern?"

"Twelve miles." The old man glared at the two riders suspiciously.

"Hear anything about a herd of Block Diamond steers coming this way?"

"Mister, we don't even allow Texas cattle here for the fear of ticks and Spanish Fever. Don't you be thinkin' you can break the quarantine."

"We're lookin' for a stolen herd," Sam said. "We ain't drivin' none nowhere."

"I tell you, if you Texans try drivin' your cattle through La Bette County, we'll shoot down every head of 'em. Mind now!"

"That's enough for me," Sam said to Skofer, and wheeling his big buckskin, kicked him to gallop back the way they'd just come.

Skofer, bouncing along in the saddle, came galloping after, holding on for dear life.

They rode at a steady lope, passing buckboards and wagons and an occasional crossroad hamlet, covering the eighteen miles in a little more than an hour.

Sam couldn't understand why anyone would euchre him into making a fool journey. What did it matter to anyone that he was out of town a few hours? Why was that time period so important?

Tiredly he turned the buckskin back to the liveryman, asking him to grain the horse and rub him down good, and with Skofer tagging along like a little dog after a big dog, strode up the street to Ira's Lunch.

Inside there was a rumble of confusion as men who expected to go off to work were not getting their accustomed service.

"Ever since Sharpsburg I been a little slow," old Ira called out, carrying the coffeepot in one hand and pegging along, pouring into each cup until the pot was empty. "Another pot of coffee, Melba," he called back into the kitchen.

"My ham and eggs?" a middle-aged business man asked nervously.

"Go back in the kitchen and get 'em." Ira grinned. "You're a lot faster on your feet than me."

"Where's Elizabeth?" Sam asked when the old veteran came by with a fresh pot of coffee.

"Wish I knew. She's always been waitin' at the door when I come over from the house."

"Not in her room?"

"No, I don't think she even slept in her bed."

"Any ideas where she'd be?"

"I don't know. The stationmaster was in earlier, and thought she'd boarded the westbound train."

Ira went on with the pot, filling the empty mugs, calling out orders to Melba in the kitchen, and attending to her occasional reply, "Hot cakes awaitin'!"

"They've got her," Sam said to Skofer.

"Ten to one, they're all gone."

"Damn it, Skofe, I believed that telegram and let her down."

"Don't blame yourself. It was your job to follow orders."

"And they knew it, too," Sam growled, punching his big fists together angrily. "Get down to the livery and rent four of the best horses you can."

"You can't outrun a train—"

"Get goin'," Sam said, searching his pockets for a dime.

He'd said, "I know it's not the best room in town, but they'll be looking for you in the hotels and rooming houses, and they'll never suspect you're on this side of the tracks."

She'd tried to read his face, but there was nothing sly or evil, only the big, soft, brown puppy-dog eyes that seemed to say, *Trust me. Help me. I'm yours.*

113

He'd walked her upstairs by the alley stairway, and opened the door to a room at the end of the hall with his own key.

"Is this your room?" she'd asked.

"Oh, no, not hardly." He'd flashed a warm smile. "I've rented it for this night only. No Veitengruber will find you, because no one but me knows you're here."

Inside, the room disclosed little except a bed, bureau, and a chair. A stained carpet covered some of the plank floor.

He didn't ask to come in or make any advances that could be considered improper. He just gave her the key and said, "Sweet dreams, my dear. I'll be thinking of you and I'll be back early in the morning."

Then he'd retreated back down the stairway into the alley and was gone.

She turned the key from the inside, checked the bed, and though it sagged and the mattress was lumpy, it looked clean and freshly made up.

Why would those Veitengrubers chase her this far? she wondered tiredly. Granted, they hated her for breaking loose, the same as they'd hated her mother and her father for breaking the rules they'd laid down to suit themselves, but to dog her down after this much time just proved how bullheaded they were.

She knew how iron-bound they were, how vindictive and mean they could be about the smallest infractions of their rules, and how quick they were to punish the offender.

They can't stay away from that farm very long, she thought as she drifted off to sleep. Maybe they'll be gone by morning.

Awakened at dawn by a tapping on the door, she asked drowsily, "Who is it?"

"Rene."

Slipping quickly into her dress and scrubbing the sleep out of her face, she turned the key and opened the door.

"Good morning, my dear," he whispered. "May I come in for a moment? I'm afraid I have bad news."

Half-asleep, she still felt a falseness in his tone and wondered what kind of game he was playing. It irritated her to be thought of as a fool, an incompetent, giggly female, and she told herself that she'd play the part of a silly fool and see what turned up.

"What bad news?"

"They've gone to the city marshal. He'll be sending out his deputies to check every possible hiding place."

"I'm innocent," she said to lead him on.

"Of course, we both know that, but you can't afford a scandal, and that's just what they want. We've not a moment to lose."

"I've got to go to work. Ira and Melba are depending on me."

"I took the liberty of leaving them a note saying you were going out of town and would be back by tomorrow for sure."

"I can't do that. It's my job."

"I'm sure they'll understand once you can tell them the truth," he said smoothly. "Besides, there are plenty of other jobs in this town."

Pulling two tickets from his vest pocket, he said, "We've got to catch the morning train before the rest of the town wakes up."

"But where are we going?" she exclaimed, confused.

"Not far. Just west to Junction City, perhaps a little farther, depending on how you feel."

"This has something to do with my father, doesn't it?" she demanded suddenly.

"Your daddy? Not really. Of course, his marrying a Veitengruber started the problem, but otherwise I'm unaware of where he is or what he's doing."

She wanted to call him a liar, but then she'd never know the scheme he'd worked out that was certainly going to end up somewhere near her father, because beyond Junction City was Arboreal Splendor, and on upriver lay the hamlet of Sylvan Grove.

"I've been saving up my money for a trip. I might as well go right now, so long as you've bought the tickets."

Taking along her small valise, she accompanied him down to the alley, and as dawn spread over the eastern horizon like an opening pink rose, he escorted her into the depot where she could sit on a golden oak bench in the waiting room.

They were the only ones in the room, and the only sound was the steady ticking of the regulator clock on the wall as the pendulum counted off the seconds and added them into minutes and hours.

"If it's on time, it'll be here in seven minutes," Armenescu said.

"Why are you doing this?" she asked curiously.

"Two reasons, my dear. You know how much I despise that arrogant family, and you should know how much I care about your welfare."

"You're very kind, but I'm trying to become an independent lady."

"You're very independent. Once you make a little money, you'll be completely free," he said seriously.

"There are few opportunities for a lady to make that much money on her own."

"You just wait." He smiled. "I'll show you how to make bankers tremble and tycoons fall to their knees."

"You're joking."

"Yes, in a way." He smiled. "But any girl as pretty and smart as you are can work miracles if you know what your goal is."

People entered the room carrying carpetbags and valises, and the stationmaster opened his ticket counter for those who hadn't bought their tickets in advance.

Among the gathering group she recognized the banker, Elijah Sark.

The train hooted in the distance and she thought, Bessie you've got about a minute to change your mind, and just walk out.

The black American 4-4-0 with its bright brasswork came chugging slowly to a stop, and Armenescu let out a sigh of relief. "Thank heaven—"

"Were you worried it wouldn't come?" she asked.

"No, I've been worrying about that Veitengruber clan coming ahead of the train." He smiled and escorted her to the passenger coach.

"I'll be back tomorrow?" she asked.

"With any luck." Armenescu nodded. "Don't worry about a thing."

"I don't worry as much as I used to since I know I can stand on my own two feet," she said firmly, just in case he was getting the wrong idea.

"You are such a sweet person," he said softly. "I know what you have been through."

She looked into his eyes and saw the message. *Trust me. Help me. I'm yours.*

It never changed.

Seeing Elijah Sark take the seat across the aisle, she asked, "Do you know him?"

"Slightly." And Rene nodded politely to Sark, who returned the nod equally politely.

A chill ran down Armenescu's spine. He knew where Basham was, but where was Loco Weed?

Bull Basham was drinking just enough to keep a neat edge to his spirit and not enough to dull his senses. He'd been given his orders and promised a bonus, and as he'd feared from the start, he was left behind to do the dirty work for a little money, whilst the nabobs went off the easy way and pulled in the big pot.

The hell with it. Sark had promised him five hundred dollars if he made a clean job of it. Nothing messy, nothing noisy, just quiet and simple.

If they'd left it to him, he'd just go out in the street with an iron bar and beat the sons of bitches' brains out. But no, they're schemers. Nothin's any good unless it's all been schemed out first, nice and dirty.

Follow the plan. Make yourself five hundred dollars in half an hour or so.

They acted as if he was too stupid, too beat-up in the head, to make his own plan.

Back-shoot, bushwhack. Sure, that's easy enough, but not in the middle of town. Too many people going to point up at that window, too many people going to be waiting at the bottom of the stairs.

Maybe Sark figured it that way. Get the job done and then let them hang Bull Basham high. Who would believe Bull Basham against the banker? Then he realized why Sark had always met with him secretly.

He never meant to pay a cent. In fact, he probably hoped they'd lynch old Bull before he got back to town with a suitcase full of greenbacks.

Oh, sure, he'd kill that big cowboy, but he might as well kill the banker, too. Pick up the money, head south towards El Paso.

118

Two birds with one bullet. He smiled at his little joke, and remembered Weed. Kill Weed. Sluice the whole damn tribe.

Better to have the big cowboy kill Sark. Then kill the cowboy and pick up the money. Maybe the cowboy could take care of Weed, too. Hard to play that trick. Too many things to go wrong.

Sark was right about keeping it simple. Do one at a time. Sark last. Because Sark would have the money.

He was on the verge of going back downstairs and watch Ira's Lunch from the street level where he could dry-gulch Sam Benbow, then skedaddle out the back door into the alley and over to Cherry Avenue before anyone could figure out what had happened, when from the upper window he saw Sam Benbow and the scrawny sidekick hurrying up the street.

Grabbing up the .44–40, he tried to get a bead on the big cowboy's back as he entered the restaurant, but it had happened too quickly for him to get set and make a kill shot.

Better to wait. Have to do it from upstairs, but he could get down the back stairway plenty fast enough. Just pull the trigger and run like hell.

Put it right through his wishbone when he comes out the door. Never know what happened to his heart. Bang! Blooey! Out for the count of a million. Toll the bell ten times.

Patiently, keeping the rifle trained on the front door of Ira's Lunch, he'd occasionally test himself by peering down the buckhorn sights, setting the front sight in the vee, right where he wanted it.

Rehearsing his moves, he told himself: Shoot. Run downstairs. Out the back door. Cross the tracks. You're home free.

He thought he heard a board creak in the back

room, but he told himself it was just his nerves and that he had to concentrate on this job all the way. There couldn't be anyone back there anyways.

He saw the scrawny little Skofer come hurrying out the door and sighted him in, thought for a moment of just knocking him down for the fun of it, and realized soon enough that if he gave any warning, Sam Benbow would never fit into his sights.

The cowboy ought to be right out.

Sam couldn't find the dime for the two coffees, so he put down a quarter and hurried to the door. Stepping out, he heard Ira yell, "Sam! Here's your change!"

Sam turned, mainly because he didn't want Ira to think he was being snotty with a fifteen-cent tip, and turning back, he saw the doorjamb in front of his nose explode into splinters, followed by the crack of a rifle.

Diving into the restaurant in a purely instinctive reaction, he immediately whirled back, realizing that he'd seen powder smoke from the window above the bank.

Charging back and drawing his .44, he fired twice at the window and raced across the street as fast as his bulldogger boots would carry him.

Running up the stairway, he heard another shot, more distant this time, and paused at the door of the front upstairs room.

Kicking the door open, he charged into the room, crouching low, expecting anything.

The room was empty.

Waiting a few seconds by the closed door that would open to the back room, he listened for telltale breathing or a footstep, but it was deadly quiet.

He kicked in the back room door and charged through, rolling to his left, his six-gun at the ready, but he could see nothing except a huge form sprawled near the back door.

He recognized the checkered suit and approached carefully, the six-gun aimed at Bull Basham's head, ready for a surprise attack, ruse or trick, but there was no rifle or weapon nearby.

Then he saw the blood on the big man's chest where a heavy slug had burst on through the massive body, tearing out a hole not quite big enough to hold the shiny derby hat lying next to a big, scarred hand.

The body was still twitching, the mouth working, the broken knuckles flexing, but the eyes were dead as corned beef.

Sam ran to the back window and looked down into the alley, only to see the hind end of a sorrel horse going around the corner.

Turning as he heard footsteps, he saw the city marshal and a deputy coming through the door.

"Drop that gun, cowboy." The marshal, a short-legged, long-waisted man, spoke with authority.

Sam eased the six-gun to the floor and said, "There was two of them."

"Two of who?" the marshal growled as the deputy retrieved Sam's six-gun, sniffed the barrel, and checked the cylinder.

"Fresh-fired, twice."

"This one tried to bushwhack me comin' out of the restaurant," Sam said.

"I heard that, but I don't see how he could have missed, and I don't see why you shot an unarmed man in the back."

"I didn't shoot him," Sam said.

"Then who did?" the marshal rasped.

"I don't know. Somebody was hidin' in here."

"I reckon you can come down to the jail and we'll talk some more on it."

"Whoever it was ran down the back stairway, jumped on his horse, and rode off," Sam protested.

"I said you're comin' with us. How do you want it? My way or the hard way?"

"I'm peaceable," Sam said, lifting his hands, "but . . ."

"But what?" the marshal asked, pushing him into the front room and down the stairway.

"I'm in some hurry to do some business."

"Whatever it is will wait. If somebody took a shot at you, you can figure that'll help you with the judge."

"Judge?"

"Course, you got to go to trial. Nobody shoots an unarmed man in the back, not in my town."

Coming out on the boardwalk, Sam saw a massing group of curious townsmen gathered at the entrance-way.

"You all right, Sam?" Ira asked.

"I'm fine," Sam replied, "but the marshal's got some kind of a problem."

"Get back, everybody!" the pudgy marshal yelled.

Suddenly from up the street came a cowboy holler crossed on a Yaqui Indian scream, and a rider leading three saddled horses came galloping full tilt down the street, forcing the crowd to press in against the marshal and Sam.

In the press of men, Sam sidestepped so that two men were wedged in against the marshal by the pressing crowd, while Sam worked his way into the street.

"Stop him!" the marshal yelled, breaking out of the men bunched against the wall, scared to death they were going to be stomped by the running horses.

"Go, Sam!" Ira yelled.

As Skofer brought the horses in close, Sam leaped into the saddle of the last of the running horses, let out his Coleman County squall, and gave the roan his head.

BLOOD TO BURN

The marshal, getting clear, lifted the six-gun in both hands, deliberately sighted on Sam's broad back, but as he squeezed the trigger to make a kill shot, old Ira fell against him.

They saw Sam twist sidewise as the slug creased his shoulder, then shift the reins over to the right hand, lean forward over the roan's neck, and turn the corner.

"You old fool!" the marshal yelled. "I could have killed him!"

"That man's a friend of mine," Ira came back at him strongly. "Better you turn in your badge and quit this town while you're able!"

9

Racing out of town, Sam felt the burn and ache of the bullet plowing up across the back of his shoulder, and thanked heaven he'd been leaning forward or the bullet would have broken his shoulder blade. As it was, he'd have a long, welted scar back there where he couldn't see it, and his arm would be some miserable for a week or so.

The roan caught up with Skofer's chestnut as the street opened up and changed into a county road, and Skofer saw the blood oozing from the slash in the back of Sam's cowhide vest.

"How bad?" he yelled as they passed a hay wagon barely moving down the dirt road.

"A no-see-um bit me!" Sam smiled reassuringly, and the two riders, each leading a spare horse on a slack line, galloped on west and held the pace until they passed by a crossroads hamlet named Willard, where Sam settled back on the roan and brought him down to a walk.

"Reckon they'll have a posse after us?" Skofer asked

as they rode along side by side, giving the horses a short breather.

"Maybe, maybe not," Sam said. "We've got some friends back there that know I'm not a back-shooter. Time to switch horses."

They stopped, checked their leathers, mounted up again. Sam's bay was a rangy half Thoroughbred, half Morgan—a horse, he thought, with bottom enough to carry him all the way to western Kansas if he had to.

"You picked some good horseflesh." Sam nodded with approval, took the lead rope of the roan, and kneed the bay forward.

"We oughta put a bandage on that wound," Skofer said, hanging back.

"Next time we'll change where there's water," Sam said.

Sam eased the long-legged bay into a controlled gallop so he wouldn't think he was in a short race, and kept them moving at a steady gait and was pleased to see the farms becoming fewer and farther between. Another hour and they'd be free of fences and could choose their own way.

Even if the town marshal couldn't raise a posse, Sam expected that he'd wire ahead to Junction City and have the law waiting for them.

Trying to remember how the country lay to the west, Sam remembered Fort Riley was slightly north on the Republican River, then on down was Junction City, where the railroads crossed to the south, and down a ways further there would be the Smoky Hill River coming up to make the junction.

"We'll bear a little south," he called over to Skofer. "No point in taking on the Eighth Cavalry and the town marshal, too."

With the farms gradually yielding to grassland, there was room to maneuver. They came to the river two miles upstream from Junction City where the water ran clear.

The riverbank, lined with black walnut trees, cottonwoods, and chokecherry bushes, was empty of people. No one had ridden along this way since the Indians left.

"We'll take a breather," Sam said, and let Skofer tether the horses so they could have a bite of grass while he went to the crossing, stripped off his coat and shirt, then washed out the long groove gouged out by the marshal's bullet.

"Let me help, Sam," Skofer said, joining him.

Soaking a clean bandanna in the water, he dabbed away at the cut until he could see the damage while Sam rinsed the blood from the shirt and the back of his vest.

"Half an inch lower and that ball would have nicked a back rib and just tore the hell out of it. You have to learn to hunch down further," Skofer complained.

"Then I'd get it in the butt," Sam chuckled. "No, thanks."

"Basham's dead?"

"Back-shot by somebody I never got a look at."

"And Elizabeth?"

"They've likely taken her off west. They'll end up in Sylvan Grove. Has to be that way."

"Sam, we can't ever catch up with the train."

"There's a chance," Sam said, studying the angle of the sun while Skofer put a makeshift bandage over the long gouge. "That train doesn't go to Sylvan Grove. The nearest stop is Ellsworth, and they'll likely spend the night there. We'll ride late and get out early, and maybe we can come close."

"How far you reckon from here?"

"We're lookin' at a hundred miles."

"Even relayin', I doubt these horses can do that much," Skofer worried.

"Maybe they can, maybe they can't," Sam said shortly. "Did you bring an extra six-gun?"

"There's a loaded .45 in your near saddlebag." Skofer nodded. "I always like to have a spare horse and a spare pistol."

"Sometimes you're downright sensible, Skofe." Sam laughed, mounting up on the bay.

"What do you think we'll find in Sylvan Grove, Cap'n?" Skofer asked pensively.

"We'll find Billy Faraday. I hope he's alive, but if he's dead, we'll find the polecats who killed him, too," Sam said, his eyes shining, his lantern jaw set tight.

After crossing the Smoky Hill River, Sam put them on a course directly into the face of the westering sun, easily holding to a straight path because the farms were so scarce, they hadn't gotten around to fencing off the open range, merely plowing a furrow to mark their claims.

The westerly course put them north of Abilene, a few miles from where Sam had driven two herds of longhorns up from Texas before the town got uppity and told the Texans to take their trade elsewhere. No Texan would go where he wasn't wanted, and accordingly the herds had moved west, on over to Ellsworth as soon as the railroad built shipping pens, and Abilene faded away into just another farm town.

Now the herds were having to go farther west to Dodge City, and Sam knew well enough from his working for the National Trail that in just a few more years the land would be fenced clear across the state, and that would finish the great drives northward, forcing Texas cattle to compete with Montana cattle for the eastern dollar.

As the sun disappeared in a purple glow on the flat western horizon, they forded the Solomon River, let the horses drink, then changed mounts. Sam hurried them off again into the gathering dusk.

He hoped they could ride another hour in the dark and maybe make an extra ten miles of the fifty they needed.

Suddenly he felt the roan stumble, hauled up the reins, and yelled, "Hold it, Skofe!"

Too late, Sam realized. They'd ridden into a prairie dog town, and Skofer's horse went down with a grunt, Skofer flying off to the ground.

Sam dismounted and ran to Skofer lying crumpled in the grass, and quickly felt for a pulse.

"You're all right, Skofe. Wake up!"

Then Sam saw in the gloom Skofer's piebald limping around on three legs. Leaving Skofer, Sam caught the piebald and looked at the right hock dangling from the broken cannon bone.

"Sorry, good horse," Sam murmured.

Quickly stripping off the saddle and bridle, Sam stood by the horse's head, patting his neck while he slowly took the Colt from its holster, cocked the hammer, and shot the good horse between the eyes.

The report echoed across the plains like a western dirge as the horse dropped.

Sam blamed himself for pushing too hard against Mother Nature, who would swat you down like a fly whenever you thought you could break the rules of common sense.

Skofer put his hand to his head and opened his eyes. "Cap'n?"

"My fault, Skofe. I led us into a bunch of prairie dog holes. Let's move off a ways and make camp."

Leading the three horses, Sam found a small clearing on a creek bank, picketed the horses, and settled down for the night.

"Bread and ham in the saddlebag," Skofer said, rubbing his neck.

"You're readin' my mind."

Sam fetched out the sack of provisions, and by the light of the moon and a million stars sparkling in the dark sky, made up a thick sandwich.

Laying his head back on his saddle as Skofer started to snore in peace, Sam figured that so far he'd managed to do everything wrong. He'd made Elizabeth mad at him and put her in jeopardy. He'd gotten himself creased, and was a fugitive wanted for murder. Then he'd ridden right into a prairie dog village in the dark, lost a good horse that just might make the difference of life or death for Billy Faraday and his daughter.

Billy Faraday's daughter was thinking of what had passed that long day, and what she might expect for tomorrow. She was worried that the Veitengrubers might possibly track her down, and that Sam Benbow would hate her for disappearing without any word.

When the train had stopped in Junction City, she'd thought they would find a hotel and stay the night there, then return to Topeka on the first train the next morning, the way Rene had outlined the plan to her at the station, claiming all they needed was to be rid of the Veitengrubers for twenty-four hours. Let the Veitengrubers turn Topeka upside down; they'd never find a clue as to where Elizabeth had gone. They'd have to give up and go back to mucking out the cattle barn.

But as the train had clipped along merrily at fifteen miles an hour over the long prairie, Rene and Elijah

Sark had talked quietly back and forth, and when the train stopped at a small community called Maple Hill, Rene said their plans had changed. He said the banker had offered him a good job in his new bank in Ellsworth, but that Sark wanted to stop and wait for the next train because he had business to take care of in Maple Hill.

The banker had treated them to an expensive breakfast of doughy pancakes and bacon and eggs fried in rancid lard.

They'd lingered in Maple Hill for two hours until the tall, hatchet-faced companion of the banker rode into town on a sorrel gelding that had been ridden almost into the ground and was all but ready to drop dead when the tall gunman dismounted and tethered him to the hitch rail.

The banker and the gunman had walked away while they talked, then the gunman had a solitary breakfast while they waited for the next train west.

In those hours, Rene had been charming as a pup in a basket and nervous as a duck in the desert. He'd tried to listen in on the banker's talks with his companion, and his eyes were on the move constantly.

She felt cross and dirty and tired, and she noticed Rene occasionally touched his left breast pocket, where she finally realized he kept a small pistol.

"What's the matter?" she asked bluntly.

"It's the change in plans. I hadn't known we'd meet Mr. Sark on the train or that he'd offer me employment in Ellsworth."

"Why should that bother you? I'd think you'd be overjoyed."

"I promised to return you safely to Topeka tomorrow. Now that we're going all the way to Ellsworth, we might be a day or so late, and you'll have to return by yourself."

"I guess I can manage to ride a train without a guide." She laughed at his pompously polite speech, which sounded to her like something he'd read in a romantic novel.

It was only when the tall gunman they called Weed had looked at her with his hard, frosty eyes that she felt in danger, but she'd reasoned that no harm could come to her while Mr. Sark and Rene were with her. She was just being silly, a weakness she despised and intended to avoid at all possible costs.

Rene had said he could make her independent, and as distasteful as he was, so long as she felt free to choose her own course, she would go along with his plan.

They'd taken the next train west as Rene had promised and arrived in Ellsworth late in the afternoon.

Rene had not attempted any untoward advances during the journey west, nor when they'd registered at the hotel. She had her privacy, and her dignity, and except for Rene's unusual nervousness during the day, she had only the vengeance of the Veitengruber family to worry about.

She did wish she knew more about western Kansas. Somewhere out this way was the town of Sylvan Grove, where Mrs. O'Banion lived, and maybe her dad did too.

Finishing her sponge bath, she put on her spare blouse and resolved to ask someone if Sylvan Grove was anywhere near close enough to visit.

Downstairs in the lobby, she found Rene pacing the floor, his eyes shifting back and forth, biting his fingernails.

Catching sight of her, he quickly put on a smile, touched his delicate mustache as if to make sure it was still there, then came to greet her with arms extended.

"How lovely you look, my dear. As fresh as a fresh-picked rosebud, and after such a hard day's journey."

"I'm not exactly a delicate flower," she replied. "Where are your friends?"

"I'm not sure if those men are friends or only business acquaintances."

"The tall one has eyes like a timber wolf."

"Yes. He's a little too earthy for my taste." Rene glanced over his shoulder. "Are you ready for supper?"

"Aren't we to meet Mr. Sark at suppertime?"

"He can find us in the dining room."

"You didn't actually see Benbow go down?" Elijah Sark asked again, because Sam Benbow was the only thing standing in the way to settling the past and establishing a solid foundation for an honorable future.

"I played him both ways, I told you. If Bull missed him, he would come up after Bull, and what he'd find would be enough to hang him."

"But you're not a hundred percent sure."

"The world ain't like banks," Weed sneered. "Nothin's ever sure, and if it was, I wouldn't like it."

"Be serious, Weed. We've got to get clear of that New Orleans bungle."

"We're close. Mrs. Utter never talked, and Billy won't ever say anything. Who else knows?"

"If someone who knows ever looks twice at those coins, they'll add it up." The banker leaned back in an oak chair in the hotel room and drummed his fingers on the table.

A year before, twenty new gold pieces had been changed into currency here in Ellsworth, and then sent on to Topeka to the First Charter Bank of Kansas.

Perhaps there had been more earlier, but Sark had only seen the twenty in the transfer box, and knew what they meant.

He'd quickly exchanged them for double eagles minted in San Francisco or Carson City, and no one was wiser, but after that, Elijah Sark's expanding business was on the brink of ruin.

From that day on, he'd made sure he saw every transfer box from the Ellsworth bank, and discovered that once a month five of the gold pieces were exchanged for currency.

Somewhere out there on the prairie, a man had a couple boxes full of those gold pieces and was living a quiet life off them.

Once he'd pieced that much together, he'd sent for Weed, but when Weed started watching the town, the coins had quit coming in. It was almost a dead end, and would have been, except that the clerk in the local bank remembered the man with the coins always kept his left hand in his coat pocket. He'd been afraid the man had a gun and meant to stick him up the first time. After that he'd gotten used to it and hadn't paid attention.

But that was enough to put the name of Billy Faraday onto the man with the gold pieces, and Weed had hunted far and wide for him, particularly towards the Oklahoma territory to the south, where most of the outlaws liked to pass the time.

Then when the coins quit coming and Billy Faraday disappeared, Sark had been terrified that the coins would be passed in a big city where eventually they would be questioned.

Once the question was asked of the New Orleans mint, they were all doomed.

Sark had dreamed of building a banking empire from the multitudes of farmers arriving from the East, especially the thousands of Mennonites arriving from Russia in absolute poverty. They would mortgage their whole homestead for just a sack of the turkey red seed wheat, of which the first arrivals had brought samples from their homeland.

But nothing could be sure as long as those gold pieces were hanging over his head like a sword ready to fall on his neck.

"Nobody looks twice at a twenty-dollar gold piece," Weed chuckled. "Maybe they'll bite it to see if it's real, but they never look at the mint marks."

"There are a lot of sharp-eyed bank tellers, Weed, and they know their business."

"We'll clean it all up tomorrow," Weed growled. "That damned Billy Faraday had me guessin' for a long time, because he always circled around and came into town from the south. But that one time when I saw him in the drugstore and followed him out of town, his luck ran out."

"And you killed him before you had the money."

"You ain't ever goin' to let me forget that, are you, Mr. Banker?" Weed replied sharply. "I told you, tomorrow we'll finish it."

"Still, we're depending on the gigolo and the stupid woman. Nothing is certain."

"Armenescu knows. That's enough for me. I'll have him for breakfast."

"Don't kill him until we get our document back."

"I can get it back. Build a little fire out on the prairie and stick his pretty face in it, he'll talk like a regular elocutioner."

"Suppose he tries to sneak out during the night? Have you planned on that?"

"I'll be sleepin' on his doorstep."

"And the girl?"

"I don't think she's goin' to go against us. Why don't you just move into her room and make sure?"

"I wouldn't mind trying that." Sark nodded, a wicked smile pursing his lips. "Once we've got that shipment safely in our hands, I'm going to teach her the ways of business, especially how to multiply."

"Then it's all settled?"

"All settled. First thing in the morning we take a surrey over to Sylvan Grove. Maybe take us an hour for the girl to find the O'Banion woman. Five minutes with her, and she'll give you the whole issue. Then you take a walk with the whoremaster, and the three of us come back here."

"Likely we can rest some on the way back." Weed grinned. "You want to show the lady some bluebonnets or johnny-jump-ups or something."

"Weed, sometimes you get the strangest ideas," Sark guffawed, thinking already of walking through the green grass with Elizabeth Faraday.

Weed, behind his grin, was thinking Sark would make a cold corpse and Elizabeth Faraday would make a very warm woman.

Weed got to his feet and said, "I could use a drink."

"I'll join you." Sark smiled.

Armenescu and Elizabeth had ordered a light supper of scrapple and cream gravy when Sark and Weed joined them in the hotel dining room.

"Sorry to be late. I was just looking over the town to see if it was suitable for you," Sark said to Armenescu.

"It's a wonderful opportunity for me." Armenescu played along with the game.

Elizabeth was about to ask the men if they'd ever heard of a town named Sylvan Grove, but out of the corner of her eye she saw Weed staring at her bosom, a mixture of disgust and lust on his face, and she suddenly saw herself not as an independent, free woman, but as a foolish victim of three powerful men whom she didn't even know.

She'd had no experience of life on the Veitengruber farm until Rene had drifted by, glib and hungry, and she'd seen then how ignorant she was of the world. When Ruby O'Banion's letter came, she'd escaped the Veitengrubers because of that, but now she wondered if any of these men could be called a friend.

It crossed her mind that Sam Benbow had tried to befriend her, and she'd pushed him away like a silly girl. Where was he now? Probably in the arms of a woman an awful lot smarter than she was.

Sam had told her to keep quiet about the letter, and she'd told Rene everything except the name of the town. Sam had been upset by that and tried to interfere in her friendship with Rene, and she'd put him off again because she thought he was being bossy.

Maybe he was right all the time. Maybe she should have showed him the envelope with Mrs. O'Banion's address on it. Maybe she should have trusted him instead of Rene, who was acting like a nervous Nellie more and more.

Certainly, she decided, cutting into the scrapple with her fork, she'd not say another word about the letter or the gold piece on any part of what she now considered to be Sam Benbow's business.

After all, Dad had said to go to him and he'd make it square.

But she hadn't been fair with Sam. She'd held out, and now she'd gotten herself lodged in a hotel far away from Sam Benbow or any other trusted friends.

She felt very much alone, and she felt a shiver run down her backbone as she caught the banker eyeing her slyly.

"Were you going to say something, Elizabeth?" Sark asked, covering up his naked lust.

"I was going to say I have never been this far west."

"It's a rich area," the banker said. "Perhaps we can explore some of it in the morning, Mr. Armenescu?"

"I'm sure Elizabeth would like to look around," Rene Armenescu agreed.

"Are there any Indians or outlaws?" she asked, keeping a distance, trying to be separate from any of the group's intimacy.

"There's no danger," Weed said. "Seems like I heard your dad was living around here someplace."

"Was?" she asked pointedly.

"Was, is, will be," the banker chuckled nervously. "Weed doesn't speak a cultivated English like you and me."

"I," she said, staring at the banker.

"I what?" he retorted, his face turning red.

"With proper usage, one says 'like I,' not 'like me.'"

"You ain't got proper English," Weed sneered at the banker.

"Indeed, we're off the subject, aren't we? We were discussing the whereabouts of your father."

"I don't see that where my father is has anything to do with anyone here," she said tightly.

"Somehow I understood that he lived in this area. . . ." the banker said. "Mr. Armenescu might have mentioned it. . . ."

"I don't remember saying anything about my father living in Ellsworth or the Smoky Hill Valley, for that matter," she replied stubbornly, realizing at last that she'd been brought here to point the way to her father, and not because of the Veitengrubers or Rene's heavy concern for her safety. No, with a sinking heart she realized Rene was in league with Sark and Weed. She was alone against the three of them.

"Tomorrow we can look around," Rene said.

"Tomorrow I will return to Topeka," Elizabeth said.

"Of course, my dear," Rene said, "but there is not so much hurry. There are many things to see out here in the West. We might even see a buffalo."

"I intend to catch the first train going east," Elizabeth said, rising. "Good night, gentlemen."

When she had gone, Sark glared at Armenescu. "You said you had her under control."

"I have, but you had to go and upset her."

"She don't know where we're going tomorrow?"

"She knows where it is. She just doesn't know that we all want to go over and have a look," Rene said weakly.

"I'll turn her over to Weed if you can't deliver what you promised."

Diners at nearby tables looked up and stared when they heard the banker's bitter, high-pitched voice.

"I'll go up right now and talk to her," Rene said, getting to his feet. "Don't worry, first thing in the morning we're all going for a buggy ride."

10

Returning to her room, Elizabeth thought she should immediately move to another hotel, find a local lawman, and explain her fears. But, what could she say? *The banker is trying to kidnap me? Mr. Armenescu has lied to me? That Weed man wants to kill me?*

What are you doing here? Why did you come? the lawman would ask.

What could she answer? *I'm a fool. I believed a liar. I didn't see the trap.*

What trap? You have come out here willingly with three men for some reason. What would that be? he would say, looking wise and smug.

They're after my father's money.

Who is your father?

I don't know. I mean, I haven't seen him since I was six years old.

And tell me again why you are traveling with three men.

I can't tell you. I don't know. I believed a story about the Veitengrubers. . . .

And who might the Veitengrubers be? the lawman would ask, and make a circle with his finger above his ear.

No, Elizabeth, she told herself, you got yourself into this mess and you can just get yourself out.

The image of Sam Benbow in the restaurant trying to talk sense to her came unbidden into her mind, and suddenly she felt a great yearning for the big, unkempt man who really only needed a good woman to press his shirts, sew on his buttons, and trim his hair.

Back and forth her mind went in confusion, afraid, angry, worried, determined, yet not fixing on any one source of strength or weakness.

Pacing the room, she noticed the coverlet was wrinkled, and remembered she'd straightened it out neatly before going down to supper.

Hurrying to her valise on the marble-topped dresser, she saw that the neatly packed clothing was disarranged.

Why had someone searched her things? She had nothing of value. Even the envelope that she had hidden so well had mysteriously disappeared while she'd been working in the restaurant.

Suddenly another vision came as a revelation into her mind. Sam baiting her, causing a commotion until old Skofer showed up, and then he just turned it off and walked out. Later on that evening she had discovered the envelope gone.

Of course. Sam and Skofer had arranged to take it. Sam had known she'd lied to him and held it back even though her daddy had told her to trust him. He'd arranged to have Skofer go in the back door while he started a tiff with her in the front.

Her first reaction was another flood of anger, until

she realized she'd brought it all on herself. If Sam hadn't taken the envelope, someone else, maybe a lot worse, would have taken it just now during supper.

Trying to sort out these thoughts without any degree of success, she heard a tapping at the door and cautiously opened it a crack to see Rene looking pale and wan despite his swarthy complexion.

"I need to talk to you, Elizabeth."

"All right, Rene. Come in. What is it?"

She started to tell him her room had been searched, then realized it was probably Rene who had done it when he'd excused himself in the middle of supper.

"What do you want?" she demanded coldly, facing him with her arms crossed over her breasts.

"Please, Elizabeth, don't be angry with me. I had no idea things would turn out this way. That's what I want to talk to you about."

"You lied about the Veitengrubers, didn't you?"

"Not at all," he said, his eyes shifting. "Why would I lie about that? I went out of my way to warn you."

"No, it was something else. Something to do with this trip or to keep me away from Sam Benbow, I can't decide which. Maybe both."

"You're completely misreading my efforts to assist you, my dear."

"What do you want? What do those other men want? You're all after something!"

"I want to tell you to be careful of those men, Elizabeth."

"Are you saying they mean to harm me?" she demanded, angry at his buttered-up phrases.

"Not exactly, my dear," Armenescu said. "I believe they want to use you to find your father."

"And you fixed it so I'd be on the same train with them!"

"No, my part is purely accidental. If I had known

what was in the minds of those two men, I assure you we'd have gone the other way."

"How do they know my dad is out this way?"

"I suppose you or Sam Benbow must have said something."

"Sam wouldn't say anything. He's a decent—"

"A decent man? Perhaps your emotions are stronger than your good sense." Rene glared at her.

"What do they want from my dad?"

"He may have discovered a treasure or robbed a bank, you don't know," Rene replied. "Will you tell me where he was last living?"

"I'm tired of your questions. If my father has some money, it's his business, not yours or mine or anyone else's."

"It's your business if he's dead," Rene said. "You're his only heir."

"Everywhere I turn, I'm up against a stone wall," she murmured. "I wish now I'd told Sam Benbow the whole story."

"Sam Benbow is a man of low character, always on the fringe of the law. His gun is for hire to the highest bidder."

"I don't believe that." Elizabeth was close to tears.

"Elizabeth, don't you see? I'm trying to tell you that I want to care for you, guard you against the brutes in the world. I want to teach you the finer things in life and make you an independent person while at the same time permitting me to go along with you as your agent and . . . husband."

"Husband?"

"I'm an awkward clodhopper when it comes to saying the things in my heart." Rene Armenescu set his spaniel eyes on hers. "I'm trying to say I'd be honored to have you for my wife."

Trust me. Want me. I need you.

The proposal was so unexpected, Elizabeth couldn't find words to express what was in her heart, which was not a yes or a no, but a plain and simple I don't know!

"Please, Elizabeth, you don't have to answer me just now. Tomorrow will be fine. I wouldn't want to take advantage of you." He smiled and gently patted her on the shoulder.

"I'll sleep on it."

"I need to know where Mrs. O'Banion lives. I believe it's quite close, and I believe Sark and Weed intend to do your father some harm. I'd like to find him first and warn him they're coming."

Trust me. Help me. I need you.

"I'm sorry," she said, denying the appeal in those soft brown eyes. "It's better if I just stay out of this business."

"You may be endangering your father's life."

"You'd ride off tonight to his hometown?"

"Indeed I would, and with your help, I believe I can save your father's life."

"I think I'll have to trust my dad's faith in Sam Benbow."

"Elizabeth!" His voice cracked. "It's not only your father who is in jeopardy, but you and I, too!"

"How can that be?"

"Those men think I know where your father is. They will kill me if I can't guide them there in the morning. If you tell me now, I'll go ahead and save us."

Elizabeth was saved from making a reply by a knock at the door.

Opening it wide, she saw tall, hatchet-faced Weed, his eyes frozen puddles, his mouth twisted.

"Everything all right, miss?" he asked, glancing at Rene.

"Yes."

"I'm standing guard tonight out here in the hall." Weed indicated the chair he'd placed between the two doors in the hall.

"Why?"

"Just in case somebody tries to bother you."

"I was just leaving," Rene muttered weakly, going out the door and on into his own room.

"Good night, Mr. Weed," Elizabeth said, closing the door and locking it from the inside.

She was trapped, and so was Rene Armenescu. No one was going to be allowed to ride ahead of anyone else.

As the prairie wolves and coyotes ceased their nightly litany, and the roosters in every backyard in the town of Sylvan Grove challenged one another for their small dominions, Ruby O'Banion rose from her lonely bed and peered out the ripply glass pane of her kitchen window at the dawn. Seeing that there would be no rain and the day fair, she started a corncob fire in her small cast-iron stove, pumped a pot of water to heat on the back lids, and cooked herself a simple breakfast of bacon and eggs with homemade bread.

Using some of the warm water heated on the stove, she first washed her face, then the dishes.

Wearing a simple gingham dress, she went out her back door and noticed that her tomatoes were ripening and the cucumbers were growing well.

Going on, she crossed over to the garden that Billy had planted and would never harvest. The potato vines were dying down and she thought, Maybe he buried it there, right in with the spuds, and resolved to start digging the potatoes that day.

There was no point in going into the small frame house. She'd searched every inch of it twice, then cleaned it thoroughly and locked the doors. She wouldn't open it up again until someone came along looking for a place to rent.

From the back of the lot in the pen of woven willow branches, the big-breasted barred Rock rooster drummed his wings on his breast, rose to the tip of his toes, and, stretching his neck as far as it would go, gave a mighty crow that sounded clear to the other end of town.

"Good boy," she murmured.

Unlocking the workshop, she went inside, took the wooden scoop from the peg, lifted the top of the barrel, leaned over, and scooped into the cracked corn.

The meadowlarks were still asleep when Sam shifted his head on his hard-shell saddle, sensing a change in the night's mood—a softening of the coyote's yell, a muting of the owl's simple taunt, a crow lifting off early, and wild pigeons commencing to dare the darkness before the hawks could fly and find a thermal.

Slipping into his boots and putting his Stetson on, he touched Skofer on the shoulder and decided to skip coffee and breakfast. He wanted to be riding as soon as he could see the ground.

He brought in the three picketed horses, who'd rested and eaten through the night. Though not as fresh as they were yesterday, they could still make another fifty miles or so.

"Oh, dear Brutus," Skofer groaned. "Did you happen to bring a pint along with you?"

"*You* loaded the saddlebags," Sam answered, lifting his hull onto the roan and tightening down the leathers.

"How could I forget it! You old devil, you're goin' to get punished for that oversight," he scolded himself. "You'll do double guard duty for the next ten days, or ride the cannon. Which do you prefer? I prefer a drink, sir," he answered himself.

"Can't you think up some kind of a ripstaver song to start the day?" Sam grinned.

"I'll try, Cap'n." Skofer scratched at the stubble on his face, then with a raspy howl, commenced singing.

"Rye whiskey, rye whiskey, rye whiskey I cry.
If I don't get my whiskey, I'll surely die!"

"Sound the attack, Sergeant!" Sam mounted up.

Skofer scrambled aboard the bay, and taking the sorrel's lead rope, followed Sam across the prairie in the first light of dawn.

Sam kept them at a walk, warming up the horses' muscles as well as giving the sun time to rise and show the footing.

They were well past the prairie dog town, but there were still boggy sloughs and cutbank gulches, old buffalo wallows half-hidden by the tall bluestem, and badger dens that would snap a horse's leg off at the knee.

"Soon as we hit the river, there'll be a trail," Sam said as Skofer came up alongside.

"Any Indians left in this country?"

"I doubt it. For one thing, the moon is wrong for them to come south, and the other thing, they're all dead or moved north."

"But you can't be sure," Skofer argued.

"What's sure is the buffalo are gone, and their Indian brothers aren't far behind."

As the sun rose, Sam kicked the big roan into an

easy gallop. Far to the west he saw a line of trees rising out of the empty green pasture.

"That's the Saline River." He nodded to Skofer, and held the pace until the roan commenced heaving for air, then he dismounted, swapped hulls, and mounted the sorrel.

Skofer, weighing hardly more than half of Sam's 180 pounds, continued on his bay.

Over the long, empty land they rode, but the trees never seemed to grow any closer.

"I know we're moving," Skofer complained, "or else I'm gettin' a sore butt for nothin'."

"I ain't felt so good since the hogs et the twins." Sam smiled, taking a deep breath of the air redolent with fresh-growing green grass and bluebonnets. "But I'm goin' to feel better when I roast the liver of whoever's hurt Billy."

Sam knew in his heart that Billy was dead, otherwise he would have countermanded his letter. He'd done the proper thing in writing the letter in the first place, and he wouldn't ever allow such a thing to cause a wild-goose chase, endangering his friends.

Army friends were different from just plain friends, he thought as the sorrel carried him smoothly over the great, grassy pasture. Army friends were more like iron rods welded together in the blacksmith's coals, forged and pounded together on his anvil. You ate together if there was something to eat, you shared if there wasn't. You faced the awful fire of muskets and rifles, cannons and mortars together. War brought you together and battle made you hard and loyal, and when it was all over, you knew who your friends were and how much they could give. The survivors never forgot, and they were a different breed of men.

That could be a bad thing if they happened to get

ahold of the wrong leader with the wrong ideas, but most times their leaders kept their minds clear and wouldn't ask a friend for a favor that wasn't right.

Especially Billy. There weren't many times he ever asked for anything. Maybe if he was lying out there in a crater bleeding to death with his hand shot off, he might just lift it up to let you know he was still alive, but he'd never yell for help or endanger the troops.

Likely he overdid it. Overdid it when he rushed into marriage. Overdid it charging when he might have been running. Overdid it when he went back up to Missouri and tried to make a life with his little family. Overdid it letting his wife back off and stay with her kin instead of just grabbing up her and the girl and riding west.

It would follow, Sam realized, that when he figured out Billy's connection with the new double eagle, he'd overdid it being a friendly person, ready to help out some poor widow woman or some such.

So when that letter was mailed, it meant business, not some little careless mistake. Billy never made careless mistakes.

And he asked Sam to make it square.

Sam intended to make it square in spades, with the joker wild.

A mile from the Saline River they cut a trail that ran east and west.

It wasn't much of a river, but it ran year-round, and the water was still clean and sparkling clear. They stopped to water the horses, and Sam swapped mounts again.

"Your bay holdin' up?" Sam asked.

"Hell, I'm not much more'n a flea on his back," Skofer said. "He'll do."

The first hamlet they happened on was Shady Bend, and that's about what it was, except for a flour mill powered by a crude waterwheel. A family lived in the back of the mill itself, and the lady there wanted to talk to someone, but Sam said he'd like some bread-and-butter sandwiches in a hurry, and after her stocky little husband made a fist, she calmed down enough to cut off some hunks of fresh-baked bread and slathered the butter in between.

Holding to the gallop, Sam and Skofer continued on upriver past a two-cabin hamlet called Sparkling River, and then held on to the trail for a long ten miles, all but finishing the horses, to Arboreal Splendor, a town with ten houses.

A general store handled all the business in town, including the post office. The problem for Sam was that the trail forked.

The owner of the store was a big-bellied German immigrant named Rosewurm, who chewed tobacco and spit on the floor as he weighed up beans from a gunnysack into smaller paper bags.

"Sylvan Grove? Ain't nothin' up there. Most folks stop over here," he said when Sam asked directions.

"We're not stopping over anywhere. We're just goin' through."

"What for you want to know where it is then?" The bulky man spit at the tail of a sleeping cat.

"Which fork goes up there?"

"We got the county seat and we're keepin' it," Rosewurm declared rhetorically.

"You can have it. We've got business in Sylvan Grove."

"What kind of business would that be? You don't look like railroaders."

"We're in a hurry, mister," Skofer piped up.

"What's the hurry, then? Sit down and have some crackers and cheese. This is a town growing so fast, it beats the grass."

"I'm goin' to ask you one more time polite, and then I'm goin' to hit you a lick that will straighten you out, mister," Sam growled.

"Hard man? Okay, hard man, take the left fork, you'll get there sooner than you think."

"Thanks, mister."

Sam strode out to the hitch rail and mounted the roan. Kicking him into a gallop, Sam took the left fork with Skofer alongside, until after a mile, he realized the trail was gradually turning south.

"He lied!" Sam yelled, reining up. "We're over three miles south of the Saline right now."

"How can you be sure?" Skofer asked, disgusted.

"Can't. We'll go over that little rise and see if there's any sign, then turn back."

Coming toward them around the small hillock, Sam saw a man riding a white mule.

An old man, weathered and worn, his overalls patched on patches, greeted Sam with a big smile.

"Good afternoon to you."

"Afternoon," Sam said. "Could you tell me where this trail goes? And I don't have time for the Arkansas traveler show."

"This trail goes from Arboreal Splendor south to Grassy Glory."

"Not Sylvan Grove?"

"No, you took the wrong fork at Arboreal Splendor."

"That storekeeper told us to take the left fork."

"That storekeeper is a mouthy son of a bitch," the old man said. "Somebody ought to break his jaw for him and dally his tongue."

"Thank you kindly, sir," Sam said, and turned the roan.

In a fury Sam kicked the tired horse back to a gallop

and rode without speaking until they arrived in front of Rosewurm's store.

"Change my saddle to the sorrel, Skofe," Sam said, swinging down and striding into the store.

He found big-bellied Rosewurm in the back of the store slicing blocks of cheese from a wheel with a long butcher knife.

Ignoring the knife, Sam leaned across the counter and, swinging as hard a right as he could muster, sent it like a fist-sized rock to the German's jaw.

Sam felt the jawbone break as the big man fell across the cheese, coldcocked.

Picking up a chunk of cheese, Sam nibbled on it for the taste, and said, "I knew it'd be rotten."

Striding back to the horses, Sam felt a hundred percent better.

"That's some better'n a hot bath," Sam muttered as he mounted the sorrel.

11

The hen clucked expectantly and the rooster hunched his wings up around his neck and stamped out a little jig around her with his head down and tail up, and coming around behind her with his calculated bluster, mounted the hen for a moment, slid off to the hard ground again, then strutted up and down the yard as the hen clucked disapprovingly and ruffled her feathers as if to let in a little air.

Ruby O'Banion leaned down into the barrel, dug with the wooden scoop into the golden cracked corn as she had been doing for a month, thinking she'd have to buy another sack of corn soon, when the scoop hit something hard.

It couldn't be the bottom of the barrel, she thought, puzzled. What could it be? Then, without even looking, she knew.

When Elizabeth left her room with her packed valise early that morning, she found not only Weed waiting for her, but Elijah Sark as well.

"Good morning, Elizabeth." Sark smiled like a toad ready to lick up a fly. "I was hoping you would rise early."

"What is it you want?" she asked with early morning exasperation.

"I have some rather distressing news, I'm afraid."

"What news?"

"Not here, please," the banker insisted, and led the way down the stairway, into the dining room.

"Mr. Armenescu?" she asked.

"A late sleeper." Sark smiled again. "He'll be along presently. He has the mistaken idea that bankers keep banker's hours."

Seated at the table with a fresh damask cloth, she asked only for a cup of coffee and a cinnamon roll for breakfast.

"It may be a long day, my dear," Sark said smoothly. "Are you sure you wouldn't like some ham and grits?"

"I'll be going back to Topeka on the next train," she said firmly. "It won't be that hard of a day."

"Perhaps after I explain the nature of our business with you, you'll change your mind." Sark stuffed his pouched mouth with ham fat, which seemed to be absorbed instantly into his swollen pink jowls.

Freshly shaven and perfumed, but with heavy, dark circles under his eyes, Rene Armenescu arrived and sat down beside Elizabeth.

"Coffee only. Black," he told the waitress, and as he waited, he drummed his fingers on the table nervously.

Seeing the deadly Weed, the cunning, merciless banker, and the stubborn Elizabeth, he felt as if he'd tried for too big a bite of the pie. He'd thought he could outmaneuver the three of them and end up a rich man, but now he thought he'd either be rich today or dead, and he didn't like the odds.

If he could have backed out, simply stood up and said good-bye, he would have done it instantly, but they had him bound by his own glibness, and he was as powerless to move as a mouse hypnotized by a snake. He carried two hideout Remington .41-caliber two-shot derringers, one in either side of his gray frock coat, but he was afraid.

The banker seemed not to care about the document he'd signed describing their dealings, seemed to know he had no one he could trust to leave it with, seemed to know he'd hidden it behind his bureau drawer, where it would never be found.

What was Sark telling the girl now?

"Let me tell you a little fairy tale which I'm afraid I must ask you not to repeat."

"I wouldn't do that," Weed interjected. "Why not just let me kill the dude slow, and then she'll see we mean business."

"Just a minute—" Armenescu blustered.

"No," the banker said, and raised his hand. "The less bloodshed the better. Maybe you could be getting your horse and the surrey ready, Weed. I'm not inclined to waste much more time."

"Be careful," Weed said, leaving the table.

"Now . . ." The banker made a steeple of his fingers and looked at the ceiling. "Some three years ago two men and a woman conceived of a plan to remove a large quantity of newly minted gold pieces from the New Orleans mint. It was a complicated, but a foolproof, plan except that an extra person was needed to actually carry the specie from the mint to a meeting place. The three met your father, who was more or less adrift in New Orleans, and though he wouldn't commit a robbery for money, he would commit a robbery to help out a woman with a long, sad story, especially if the robbery was planned so that no one could get hurt in any way—"

"You were one of the three, and Weed, too," Elizabeth interrupted.

"Let us say that's true. Then let us say your father made two very bad mistakes. First, for whatever reason, he killed the woman. Secondly, he ran with the gold. He ran very far and he covered his tracks well."

"How did you find him?" Armenescu asked.

"Along the way, using various tricks of the trade, I was able to buy a small bank in Topeka.

"Then twenty of those gold pieces turned up in this town and were sent on to Topeka. They are unusual because they have never been circulated. Your father took the entire issue. Not only that, but the New Orleans mint hadn't produced double eagles since 1861, and they haven't minted any since the robbery. Cashing in those gold pieces in Ellsworth was your father's undoing. They were very noticeable, especially if you knew what to look for. After that, he'd cash in a few every month regularly."

"So you set a trap for him."

"He was extremely clever and not all that easy to trap, because, first of all, he lived a considerable distance from Ellsworth."

"You and Weed killed him because he wouldn't tell you where it was—" Elizabeth said angrily.

"No, no, my dear. I abhor bloodshed. To be perfectly frank, dear child, your father died of a heart attack. His health was frail, and his spirit seemed to welcome death."

"He was a good man who seemed to do everything right, but it always came out wrong," she said softly.

"I have some of that problem myself." Armenescu nodded.

"You couldn't even shine his boots," Elizabeth retorted. To the banker she said, "Is that all of your fairy tale? If it is, I'm leaving."

"No, not yet, my dear. It seems your father left a letter that was mailed to you."

"How do you know about that?" she demanded, then turned to Armenescu. "Did you tell him?"

"No, my sweetheart," Armenescu replied, "I have told this man nothing."

"But you're all working together, aren't you?"

"After a fashion, but Mr. Armenescu is not nearly as important to us as he might think." The banker smiled again.

"Then how did you find out about the letter?"

"You put your trust in strange places, sweet child."

Elijah Sark removed the two letters from his coat pocket and handed them over to Elizabeth, whose face turned pale with shock, which was exactly what the banker expected.

"So you see, my dear, Mr. Benbow is my informant."

"I still don't believe it!" Her voice broke with disappointment.

"I think you'd better believe in the evidence right in front of your eyes."

"You snake!" she cried out, and as nearby customers looked across at her, Sark held up a cautionary hand.

"Be very careful, Miss Faraday, if you care anything about Mr. Benbow. Now we shall be leaving. Mr. Weed will be waiting."

"Where are we going?" she asked in a daze. Sark had hit her with everything he had, and she couldn't

156

absorb so much punishment in such a little space of time.

Her father a murderer of a woman?

Sam Benbow giving away her letters?

Rene Armenescu only a slicker trying to pilfer the sugar bowl?

Too much, too much! Too much for one little country girl.

Escorting her down the steps from the veranda, the banker directed them to a surrey where Weed, mounted on a strong buckskin, waited.

"Will you handle the reins, Mr. Armenescu?" The banker smiled his vulture smile as he helped Elizabeth step up and take the rear seat.

Once the banker was seated beside Elizabeth, and Armenescu had the reins to the pair of chestnut geldings, Weed asked, "Which way?"

"Miss Faraday can tell us that," Sark said benignly.

"You don't know?" she flared back.

"We're fairly sure we can find it, but you can make it easier."

"Why didn't you ask Sam Benbow?" she came back strongly.

"It slipped my mind," Sark said. "I didn't expect you to make our journey more difficult than it is."

"It was on an envelope . . ." she said, as if confused and trying to remember.

"I'm tired of wasting time. Take the road north, Armenescu," the banker snapped, taking a small .36 caliber Colt from his briefcase and folding his arms so that the small Colt was concealed with the barrel pressed into Elizabeth's right side.

No one on the street saw anything unusual about the porky rich man pompously sitting with his arms crossed and staring straight ahead.

Armenescu slapped the reins on the horses' rumps, and with Weed riding alongside, they took a side street off toward the wagon road that went north into the nearly unspoiled Big Pasture.

When they had cleared the last house and nothing but the great plain lay before them, Sark said, "The name of the town, please."

"I'm trying to remember. I lost the envelope." She stalled for time.

"Don't lie or I shall burn Mr. Armenescu alive before your eyes. I admit he's not much, but still, he's a human being."

"And what are you?" she demanded, her voice going shrill.

"I am a man looking for the money your father stole from me. And I promise you, I will have it before the sun sets or you will be wishing you were dead."

"It was a strange name," she said, catching sight of a bit of blue in the green grass, added, "It was a flower. Yes, I remember now. Bluebonnet, Kansas."

"I never heard of it," the banker growled. "You, Weed?"

"Me neither."

"Watch them, Weed." Sark returned the Colt to his briefcase and brought out maps of Ellsworth County and Lincoln County to the north. Each city, town, and hamlet was named on the maps, and Sark studied both maps for a few minutes, and shook his head. "She's lying, Weed. You want to see if she'll talk to you?"

"I'd like that just fine. . . ."

Weed rode the buckskin close to the surrey and bent over as if to lift Elizabeth out of the surrey, into his arms.

She pushed against the banker, evading Weed's hand.

"Wait a moment," she said quickly. "Sam Benbow told me not to tell you."

"Why would he say such a foolish thing?" the banker asked.

"Sam said he wanted to be there waiting for you. Him and a bunch of his friends. I don't want to be in the cross fire."

"What an imagination!" Sark said coldly. "You have two seconds to tell me that name, or you're going for a ride with Weed you'll never forget."

"Why don't you say something, Rene?" she cried out frantically.

"Tell him the name, Elizabeth. There's no other way." Armenescu looked over his shoulder, and she saw the fear in his eyes. "Maybe later on they'll turn us loose."

"Why would we want to keep you?" the banker laughed. "Your time is up. Weed!"

"Come here, sweetheart, I'm goin' to show you the elephant!" Weed laughed, bending down again.

"All right!" she cried out. "It's a place called Sylvan Grove. That's all I know."

"That may be enough, my dear," Sark said, studying his maps again. "Yes, there it is in Lincoln County up the Saline River from Arboreal Splendor."

Then we're on the right road," Weed said. "It'll be another fifteen, twenty miles."

"You promised to turn us loose, don't forget," Elizabeth said, trying to compose herself and get her head to working again.

"You have my solemn promise," the banker said calmly, lighting a fat cigar and looking about the empty prairie as if enjoying the excursion.

Mrs. O'Banion scooped the cracked corn out of the barrel into a bushel basket until she could see the lid of a tin box bound in brass. Brushing aside the loose corn, she read the stenciled inscription:

U.S. MINT
GOVERNMENT PROPERTY

She tried to lift the box out and found it was so heavy, she had to lay the barrel on its side in order to drag it free.

A brass padlock through a heavy cast-brass hasp secured the lid of the box, and then she remembered the key ring with the brass keys hanging behind the stove.

Trying to walk nonchalantly, she left the workshop and strolled through the back door of the house, knowing for sure someone was spying on her, then, dropping the keys in her apron pocket, she took the broom from the corner, came out on the porch, and swept her way down the stone path to the workshop again, hoping that the watchers would approve of her tidiness.

Closing the door behind, she unlocked the box, lifted aside a piece of waxed paper, and saw rows and rows of bright gold pieces. She ran her fingers over the faces dreamily, and picked out a handful to clink in her hand as she thought of all the things she'd wanted to do in her life but had never ever gotten started because of the way the cards had been dealt. But now the dealer had given her four aces, and if she didn't drop the cards, she could win the whole damned pot.

Maybe there was another box of coins in the oats barrel too . . . ?

She saw herself in a full, flowing silk dress being driven down a boulevard by a black driver dressed in red and gold, nodding to the other ladies in their fineries. She saw herself in an elegant dining room with a huge crystal chandelier hanging from the ceiling over a long table with a white cloth and china dishes with all the right silver and wineglasses, and all the ladies in their fineries nodding at her as she lifted a delicate tulip glass to toast her good fortune.

She saw herself on a great white steamship dressed in a flowing silk gown and carrying a ruffled silk parasol, waving good-bye from the broad deck to all her friends in their fineries down on the dock.

She saw a gentleman in elegant attire wearing a Prince Albert coat and silk top hat approach and bow. "Would you care to dine with me, Madame?"

She shook her head to bring her mind back to reality, then, knowing she was spending too much time in the workroom, time that the watchers would be counting, she replaced all the coins but one, slid the box back into the barrel, righted it, and poured the basket full of cracked corn back over the top.

She'd have to buy a sack of corn from the miller very soon, she realized.

But before anything else, she had to think.

"Oh, Billy . . ." she sighed as she saw the monumental task ahead.

A knocking on the feed room door broke her reverie.

"Who is it?"

"It's me, Mrs. O'Banion. Sophie Santee. I was just wonderin' if you was all right. . . ."

"Why wouldn't I be all right?" Ruby O'Banion asked harshly, opening the door and seeing her neighbor with the pinched face and pointed nose trying to look stupid while her foxy eyes were spying into the workshop.

"We'll, I was puttin' out my wash and seen you go in, but not come out, and I thought, my stars, she's been in there a long time! Maybe she had a stroke or fell, and I just thought what harm would it do if I just come over to see if you was all right."

"How do I look?" Ruby asked. "Get on back to your washtub, and pray for your sins. I don't need no watchdog lookin' after me or my business."

"Well, my stars! You didn't need to get so high and mighty just because I'm bein' neighborly. Whatever was takin' you so long, Ruby?"

"I got a man hidin' in the feed barrel here, Sophie. If I don't give him service about every hour, he gets mighty nervous."

"I never can understand you, Ruby O'Banion!" she sniffed. "I seen you with that Billy feller and knowed it wasn't proper, but you didn't hear me sayin' a word against you."

"No, you were talkin' about somebody else," Ruby declared angrily. "I know you got a hole in your curtain you peek through all day. I'd think you'd get a sore neck."

"Well, I declare! The wicked flee when no man pursueth, is what the Scripture says!"

"Who's fleein'? I wish the hell I could, old lady. Oh, how I wish I could!"

"Course, we'd do you the favor of buyin' you out if you ever feel the need."

"You wouldn't pay me enough to get me to Shady Bend," Ruby snorted, and shook her fist at the pinch-faced woman in frustration.

"What you doin' with those keys, Mrs. O'Banion?" Sophie Santee asked in a taunting and triumphant voice.

Ruby couldn't help but flush, and quickly said, "I'm goin' to put a lock on the door to keep my neighbors from stealin' my goods."

"I swear, Ruby, you're a-blushin'!" the woman

cackled with glee, and turned to go back to her own yard.

Ruby stared after her, knowing how shrewd her mean little mind was, trying to think of how much she'd guessed.

If she was goin' to get that gold out of there, she'd have to do it in the dark of the night.

She'd need a team and a buckboard to drive over to Ellsworth and change those coins into greenbacks.

She wondered how much would a buckboard and a couple of good horses cost.

More than one gold double eagle.

What she'd do, she decided, was wait till dark, take a handful of those gold pieces, then at daybreak walk the twenty miles over to Ellsworth, and buy everything she needed to get out of Sylvan Grove in a hurry.

But then, she thought, even if I leave this place for one day, they'll be swarmin' all over, pokin' into everything. Sophie Santee would be the first one to break the locks on the workshop.

"Oh my, Billy, what can I do?" she said out loud, with tears in her eyes.

A mile outside Arboreal Splendor, the roan came up lame. Sam dismounted, lifted the near front hoof, and saw he'd cast his shoe, the clinched nails tearing a dollar-sized chunk of hoof off as it broke loose.

"Want me to lead him in?" Skofer asked.

"Skofe, I don't think we have a minute to waste. He'll either follow along or somebody will steal him. I'm not goin' to worry about it."

"For sure he won't starve to death," Skofer said as Sam saddled the sorrel who had been ridden about as far as he could go.

"Sorry, horse," Sam said, kicking the weary horse up to a slow canter, which he could only sustain a few minutes and then started to falter back to a slower gait.

Sam knew he had the choice of whipping the horse on and probably ruining him forever, or he could let him walk and see if he could even make it to Sylvan Grove.

"You're right, Skofe," Sam said, "but we're not stopping."

He dismounted from the wheezing sorrel and, with the bridle reins in his hand, started walking, leading the blown horse.

"Sam, we ain't never going to get there walking," Skofer objected.

"What else is there?" Sam asked grimly.

"S'posing I ride on in to Sylvan Grove and find another horse and bring him back here?"

"Skofe, there could be a lot of trouble if Sark and Weed get there before we do."

"I'll be careful." Skofer nodded his head vigorously.

"No, Skofe, you've got to be smart, too. They've got Elizabeth somehow, and when Billy said make it square, he meant for me to look after the girl, not get her killed."

"I'm listening," Skofer said seriously.

"You've got to go in quiet like, lookin' like a cowboy out of work. If them people look nervous or spooked, you just turn around and get back here. Otherwise, you hope there's a livery stable will rent you a horse."

"And if there ain't a livery?"

"Do your best." Sam dug out his poke and handed it up to the old man. "Spend it all if you have to, but do it fast, don't stand around all day."

"Yes, sir, Cap'n," Skofer said soberly, saluted, and

kicked the bay into the same slow canter Sam's sorrel couldn't do.

Leading the tired horse whose strength was slow in coming back, Sam reflected that old Skofer would probably ride right down the middle of Main Street into an ambush.

That Weed jasper wasn't so awful shrewd, but Sark more than made up for it.

Why had Elizabeth gone off with them? Why didn't she trust him? How could she have any faith at all in that slimy critter Armenescu?

"Billy . . ." Sam said out loud to the sky or grass or the horse or his own vision of Billy wearing his kossuth hat with the long, curly feather, "Billy, I recall the day we happened to get mixed up and rode into Sheridan's scouts, and then we was runnin' for our lives when the gray horse missed his jump and fell. . . .

"Billy, I remember I was tryin' to catch that gray horse and get to runnin' again, and you turned your chestnut around on a dime, put the reins in your teeth, and charged the yellow legs with a revolver in your left hand and your saber in the other, squallin' like a Comanche with his butt caught in a crack . . . and you give me just enough time to get up on that gray and then we gave them a dash that'd make a man still proud rememberin' how strong and good we were then. . . .

"Well, Billy, I don't feel so strong and good any-more. I been makin' mistakes and I'm goin' slower and the luck is not so plenty as it was.

"But," Sam said, trudging along with his eyes on the ground, "it ain't so much what we been as what we are, and I guess I'm still game."

12

Nervous as he was, still Rene Armenescu believed he would not only survive this day, but end up possessing a fortune in double eagles.

His two loaded derringers remained snugly hidden inside his fitted coat, and with the open prairie so vast and rich, his spirits were on the rise, and it seemed impossible that he should be slated to die on such a grand day.

The team moved along willingly as Weed set the pace at a fast trot, yelling at the team occasionally, "Pick it up! Pick it up!"

All Rene Armenescu had to do was hold the reins and listen to Elijah Sark tell Elizabeth how clever he was.

Armenescu wondered if the old goat thought he could charm her clothes off. No fool like an old fool, he thought, as he envisioned himself charming her into his own embrace. Given a little unfettered time, he knew he could do it, because she was no different from any other silly female trying and failing to keep the show of modesty while deep inside they were all hellcats who would do anything to get a man under control.

They all wanted to put the collar around a man's neck and walk him up and down the street like a cut tomcat, saying, "Look at what I've got!"

All he'd ever done was reverse the process. Let them think they had the halter tightened up tight, and all of a sudden they find they've got to earn it.

"Yes, my love, I'm all yours. I'm going to make a celebrity out of you. With your beauty and talent, I'll make you into a Salome or Lily Langtry. Of course, I'll have to share your favors with a few of the impresarios and people in the theater business, and maybe a few ranchers and a couple hundred Mexican cowboys. . . ."

Armenescu smiled as he rehearsed his little joke, but then he heard the banker saying, "Two thousand three hundred twenty-five double eagles. Do you know how much that is?"

"It must be a lot!" Elizabeth forced herself to give the fat-wattled banker a warm smile, her expression demure and interested at the same time.

"A thousand double eagles is worth twenty thousand dollars, face value. Two would, of course, be forty thousand dollars. And there's still three hundred twenty-five left over."

"My goodness!" Elizabeth smiled. "You can buy a mansion with that much money!"

"When I get my hands on that money, I can buy you everything you ever dreamed of."

"A big white house with big elm trees," she said dreamily, "and a red and black buggy with shining brass lamps and a pair of matched black horses . . . Oh, wouldn't that be fun!"

Weed looked at Sark with disgust, thinking the old

crook believed he was making time with that girl, and she was just feeding him enough taffy to choke him.

He reflected that, after all, it did no harm to humor the old bastard, because as soon as that gold came into the open, that old horse was going to the pasture in the sky, and Mr. Big Stud Loco Weed was going to pack those two boxes to El Paso and tree the town. He reckoned he could kill the three of them in less than two seconds, and he'd try to make it in one.

"Unfortunately the world will never know what genius it took to remove over two thousand double eagles from a U.S. mint with only Weed and your father knowing about it. Sheer genius!"

"How did you ever figure it out?" Elizabeth gazed at the porky banker with wonder.

"I was working as an accountant in the mint, and Weed was a patrolling guard. After we became acquainted, we learned that we both wanted the same thing."

"Money . . ." she breathed.

"Exactly right, my dear. It took me six months to find the key person in the mint, a Mrs. Utter. She controlled not only the inventory, but the keys to the vault."

"And how did you charm her into your plan?"

"I discovered her husband was a philanderer and abused her badly. I gave her my sympathy. We planned on escaping to Florida as soon as we could afford to, and live out our lives in paradise."

"But there was never enough money for the dream, was there?" Elizabeth nodded sympathetically.

"How astute you are, my dear. Then one day I noticed the New Orleans mint was to resume minting double eagles—something that had not occurred for eighteen years." He paused. "Perhaps after this sad affair is over . . ."

"Perhaps . . ." she said, batting her blue eyes, "but how could you ever get so much money out of such a heavily guarded building?"

"It was a masterpiece of bookkeeping. Mrs. Utter simply used a pair of scissors to excise all mention of that issue, and as issues go, it was quite small, so that it could be overlooked. I did my part by making the proper entries in our ledgers, which accounted for the gold bullion used to make the coins. Mr. Weed saw that two boxes with the proper markings were deposited in the darkest corner of the vault."

"Those boxes were full of gold?"

"No, my dear, a hundred years from now, someone will open one of those boxes and find a lot of horseshoes!" Sark chuckled and patted her knee.

"So it was like an illusion."

"Exactly. Mrs. Utter doctored her books to make the coins disappear. I doctored my books to make the bullion disappear. Weed brought the entire coinage into Mrs. Utter's office and stored it in her coat closet."

"But why did you need my father?"

"You're talkin' too much!" Weed interrupted, riding up close.

"It's no harm now," Sark retorted, feeling proud of himself and wanting to preen his feathers. He'd always wanted to explain how clever he'd been in organizing the robbery that was so secret, no one even knew it had taken place.

"We needed a man to just come with a hand truck and carry the boxes to a buckboard down the street, because we wanted to be at our position in case something went wrong at the last minute."

"So you'd be safe from harm and no one would suspect you!"

"Yes, it was set up perfectly. The only flaw was your father. He was a dishonest man."

"What a shame," she said. "I never really knew him."

"He spoiled my masterpiece. Instead of taking the issue to our rendevous, he stole it and ran."

"After all that planning," Elizabeth commiserated.

"But we'll have it all back in a short time, my dear, and then we shall dance the light fantastic, eh?" He touched her cheek and chuckled so that a bead of saliva escaped down the corner of his lips.

"And Mrs. Utter?"

"Unfortunately, she became hysterical when she heard the bad news, and Weed—"

"Leave me out of it, Sark!" Weed yelled.

"Mr. Weed is most modest. In any case, Mrs. Utter had to be . . ."

"Put to sleep," Elizabeth said softly.

"Exactly!" the banker crowed. "I couldn't have said it any better!"

"And what a pity you had to go to all that trouble for nothing."

"Your father gave us a good run for our money, right, Weed?" Sark laughed at his joke.

"The son of a bitch," Weed said harshly. "We trusted him!"

"And did you kill him, too?" Elizabeth asked softly.

"No, no, Elizabeth," the banker assured her, patting the back of her hand. "No, he died of a heart attack. Sad to say, he was taken from us before he could tell us where he lived."

"Taken from us!" Weed exploded. "Jesus Christ, Sark, where you gettin' that kind of mealymouth talk?"

"There's a river," Armenescu announced, looking off ahead.

Weed turned his horse and said, "That's it. The town is over on the other side."

"Have you anything to tell us that will make our business easier?" Sark's warm manner faded under the pressure of the upcoming negotiations.

"I've never been west of Topeka," Elizabeth said, "and you have the letters."

"Still, we may need your help. I hope you will cooperate."

"Like Sam Benbow?"

"Exactly, Elizabeth, my dear. We don't want any more violence and heartbreak. All we want is what is rightfully ours."

Fording the river, Armenescu felt his heart tightening. Each minute brought the critical moment closer. They thought he was unarmed and a fool, a fop, a dandy, not realizing that he'd come up from the New Orleans waterfront, not realizing he'd had the simple coat tailored especially to conceal the two derringers. And, he thought, all I need is one with a heavy slug in either barrel.

They didn't realize he had worked with those derringers until he could pop them out of their spring clips like lightning striking.

Crossing the shallow river, he thought now would be a perfect time to kill them both, but then he remembered the gold. Let them find it for him first. Then take it. Take the girl. Take it all. High, low, jack, and the game!

The town, a short block of businesses in unpainted buildings, sat on a rise above the river, and the dwellings, parched and mean, clustered on down the slope.

"The damned fools are still waiting for the railroad," Weed laughed, and rode ahead to the simple main street cluttered with desiccated horse manure and sleeping dogs.

Seeing the old man sitting on the stoop of the general store whittling shavings from a soft pine stick, he pulled up and said shortly, "Where's Ruby O'Banion's house?"

The old man carefully shaved off another curl of pine, spit a gob of ambeer off to the left, then said, "Who be you?"

"Goddammit, I asked you a question!"

A boy in short pants looked out the front door of the store as the tall, thin man stood in his stirrups and pulled his big Colt.

The boy ran back into the store, out the back door, and down the alley toward Ruby O'Banion's house.

"That's right, you did." The old man didn't look up. "But I don't rightly remember."

The shot kicked dust out of the plank by the old man's boot, and he jerked backward, trying to fade into the corner of the doorway.

"Ruby O'Banion!" Weed's voice crackled with anger.

"Yes, sir," the old man stuttered. "I'm a little deef, you know. . . . Her house is down the hill. You pass the schoolhouse on the corner, turn right, and it's the next to the last house."

Feeling all-powerful and all-mighty with the heavy Colt in his hand, Weed kicked the gelding into a stiff trot, leading the way to Ruby O'Banion's house.

Warned by the boy, Ruby waited by the window with her door shut and her two-bore twelve-gauge loaded with double-ought buckshot.

By now she believed the hidden gold was hers and hers alone, finders keepers, and she intended to fight for it.

She saw the tall rider with the bulging jaw and the hatchet face stop at the picket fence, and then the surrey coming up behind.

"Mrs. O'Banion!" the rider called, dismounting and tethering the horse. "Mrs. O'Banion, you home?"

"Get on away from here, whoever you are!" she called back.

"We come a long ways to talk to you," the fat man called as he climbed out of the surrey.

"I've got my shotgun on you," she yelled. "Leave me be!"

"We have come to talk business, not to harm you," the fat man in the expensive suit called.

"Like you talked business to Billy? Cuttin' and burnin'?"

"We're old friends of Billy's," the fat man replied, "and this is his daughter."

"Lord help us," Mrs. O'Banion murmured, knowing it was going to be harder than she'd expected.

From the open window she could see the tall one moving slowly up the walk while the fat man kept on talking.

Purposely aiming high, she touched a trigger.

The blast nearly knocked her over backward, but as she peeked out the window, she saw the tall one had skedaddled back to his horse.

"I don't think you want to shoot Billy's daughter," the fat man called out, and put his small Colt into Elizabeth's side, saying, "Go ahead of me. All we want is our money. Tell her that."

"They say that all they want is their money," Elizabeth called out, and moved reluctantly to the open gate, with the banker close behind.

"There ain't no money!" Ruby O'Banion yelled back.

* * *

173

Skofer heard the revolver shot, and then a couple minutes later heard the boom of the shotgun. Spurring his tired horse up the slope, he came to the main street where a group of townsmen dressed in gray and black were huddled off by the store. Skofer noticed there wasn't a six-gun amongst them, and they sure had no inclination to get into a fight.

"Whereaway?" he yelled, not stopping.

A bearded old geezer pointed down the street, and Skofer had to decide whether to go back for Sam or go help the O'Banion lady.

He decided that for the moment, he'd try to scout the enemy first, then get back so that Sam could make up a battle plan.

Walking the tired bay down an alley, Skofer met Weed coming the other way.

With a fresh horse, Skofer might have tried to whirl away, but his bay had nothing left, and he had no choice except to draw against the gunfighter.

Weed was surprised to see Skofer coming at him, but he was ready for any kind of action, and without hesitation, palmed his forty-five and fired before the old man could get his six-gun clear.

Skofer felt a mule kick him in the head, and then it was a long falling, all downhill.

Downriver Sam heard the scattered shots and knew full well that Skofer would get himself tangled up instead of bringing him back a fast horse.

"Did my best for you, horse," he said sympathetically, mounting the weary sorrel, "but you're goin' to have to prove what you're made of today."

Whacking the reins against his flank and touching him with his spurs, Sam got the message through to the horse that he was going to have to give it his all.

Plunging forward, the big horse got himself started

and Sam held the reins closely, keeping him going straight and steady. In a quarter of a mile, the sorrel's breath was coming short and rough, but Sam wouldn't let him rest.

Hearing another shot, he thought, That'll be Skofer gettin' himself all banged up, and set his jaw as the horse lurched on ahead, coming up the killing rise that would lead directly into town.

With his head lowering and his legs moving clumsily, the big sorrel carried Sam at a near gallop to the deserted main street.

Swinging down from the blowing, spraddle-legged horse, Sam ran for the shelter of the first storefront, then worked quickly store by store, down the street.

Holding the shotgun at the ready, Ruby O'Banion faced the girl at the front door.

"Girl," Ruby said, "these must be the same men that killed Billy."

"All we want is the money," the banker said before Elizabeth could answer.

"I told you there ain't no money. Now, leave this girl alone and get on out of here!" Mrs. O'Banion said fiercely.

"We're coming inside," Sark said. "Any tricks, and this young lady will get a bullet through her back. We mean you no harm, but we won't be stopped."

Ruby O'Banion backed clear of the door, afraid of hurting Elizabeth, but not believing a word of the banker's promise.

Backing slowly toward her back door, she tried to hold the shotgun ready to fire if he tried a shot at her.

"Oh, look out!" Elizabeth cried out, staring over Ruby's shoulder.

Before Ruby O'Banion could turn to see the danger, Weed brought his six-gun down, breaking her right wrist.

The shotgun discharged both barrels into the floor and kicked clear.

"Much better," Sark chuckled, his little pouch mouth squeezing together in what he thought looked like a smile instead of the butt of a bull going uphill.

Mrs. O'Banion felt dizzy, and holding her wrist with her left hand, slumped into a kitchen chair.

"Where's the money Billy hid out with you?" Weed growled impatiently.

"Don't tell them," Elizabeth said. "They'll kill us both if they ever find it."

Ruby O'Banion bit her lip to keep from crying from the pain in her wrist, and shook her head silently.

"Where's the dude?" Weed asked, suddenly alert.

"Right here, Mr. Weed. Any trouble?" Armenescu asked, coming in the front door.

"Stay where I can see you," Weed growled.

"Did Billy live here with you?" Sark asked Ruby O'Banion.

"No."

"Where did he live?"

She shook her head stubbornly.

"I like fire." Weed lifted the lid on the stove, and seeing the glowing coals left from breakfast, smiled. "Fire is the greatest gift given a man who wants information."

"He will put your hand in that stove in ten seconds if you don't tell the truth," Sark said emphatically.

"You're the one that burned Billy's arm off?" Mrs. O'Banion sobbed, eyeing Weed.

"First I burnt his wooden hand off, then I just kept feeding him into the fire. Trouble was, the son of a bitch died before I could get past his elbow."

"You're evil, all evil!" Elizabeth said, her face pale with shock. "You tortured my father to death!"

"I had a good time doin' it, too." Weed growled. "Now, where's Billy's place?"

Taking Ruby's left hand, he dragged her toward the stove.

"I don't know nothing," she sobbed. "I just mailed a letter for him."

"The neighbors have heard all this," Elizabeth said. "They'll be coming with their guns."

"Watch the front, Armenescu," Sark said, and stepping forward to face Ruby O'Banion, he saw the telltale bulge in the pocket of her apron.

Quickly he grabbed the double eagle out of the open pocket, and holding it up to the light, laughed.

"Doesn't know nothin', does she, Weed? Burn her hand off and then we'll listen to her story."

Weed slowly jammed the hand down into the firebox of the cookstove, and Ruby O'Banion's scream could be heard clear up to Main Street, where Sam was trotting from one doorway to the next.

Hearing that scream, he knew where he was going, and ran down the alley.

Midway he came across Skofer lying next to a broken wagon box. Kneeling beside the still form with the arms flopped askew, Sam looked at the pallor, the head wound, and put his ear to Skofer's bony breast.

"I knew you were too tough to kill. . . ." Sam smiled briefly, then hurried on down the alley.

It smelled like meat burning in the kitchen.

"He lived next door," Mrs. O'Banion mumbled weakly.

"The money?"

"He gave me that coin. That's all I know."

"You found it, didn't you?" Sark pooched out his mouth.

"No . . . he gave me that coin for mailing the letter." She lied desperately, believing that Elizabeth was right. Once they had the money, they'd leave no living witnesses behind.

"C'mon," Weed growled, and dragged her by her long red hair out the back porch and across the yard to Billy's little house. Keeping Elizabeth under his gun, Sark forced her to follow along while Armenescu brought up the rear.

Crouched behind the old wagon box, Sam saw them coming out into the yard, saw that the redheaded woman was hurt, saw that Sark had Elizabeth under the gun, and tried to think of what they were planning. Certainly they were after Billy's gold, but where?

Sam watched them force the two women into the other little house and then slipped between the chicken pen and the workshop, with the wagon box behind him. Whatever he did, he had to do it right. There'd only be one chance, and if they downed him, they'd down the women too.

Sam could hear muffled voices coming from the back porch, but he couldn't understand what they were saying.

Dammit, now he was boxed in, and he needed space.

Crouched in shadows, he waited for a chance to move.

"Where is it, you cussed bitch?" Weed snarled, twisting Ruby's right hand near the break.

"I think . . . I'm goin' to faint," Ruby said, her mind going into a dizzy spiral.

"No you don't!" Weed slapped her face hard twice.

"I can't—I can't take any more. . . . Let us go . . . please. . . ." she begged.

"You can go as far as you want soon as you talk." Weed kept hammering at her.

She looked down at her dangling right wrist and her charred left hand, tears running down her face, and thought, What difference does it make, Ruby? You're not goin' anywhere anyway. . . .

"The workshop," she said, her eyes lifting and staring off into space, her voice coming out hollow and vagrant, like a voice from the cellar.

"Maybe it's a trick," Sark cautioned Weed, who was striding toward the plank door.

Rene Armenescu heard the fatal words and knew his time had come. He was behind both Weed and Sark, and he would never have another chance as good as this one.

As he drew his two derringers, Ruby O'Banion slowly turned around with her ruined hands lifted, her eyes blank, her mouth a twisted grimace, and staggered clumsily away toward Armenescu, blocking off both Weed and Sark for one vital moment.

"Watch it!" Weed yelled as Armenescu fired, his aim shaken by Ruby O'Banion's blind lunge. His bullet split her rib cage, and Armenescu dived clear of her. Armenescu threw one wild shot at Sark an instant before Weed's heavy slug broke through his high cheekbone, driving bone fragments through his brain and out the back of his skull, leaving a gaping crater big as a fist.

"Goddamn! Thanks, old lady!" Weed let out his breath.

"The little snake damned near had us both," the banker wheezed, and recovering his confidence, said to Elizabeth, "Go ahead, my dear, let's look in the workshop."

From Sam's angle of vision, Elizabeth was between him and both men as they approached the small shed.

"You're animals!" Elizabeth cried out.

Sam's single thought was to separate Elizabeth from

the two gunmen and set her free, but with her serving as a shield for them, he could not possibly start a gunfight at such close range.

Holstering his six-gun, he lifted the broken hickory wagon tongue, hoping some sort of diversion would give him a moment to throw the heavy timber at both the gunmen, knocking them down at best, slowing them down at the least.

The banker stepped forward with the brass key and unlocked the iron padlock on the hand-wrought hasp that Billy'd spent extra hours making strong and foolproof.

As the padlock clicked open, Mrs. O'Banion got slowly to her knees and screamed, "Stay out of there! That's Billy's!"

Even as she cried out, blood choked her throat and she fell back again, her body convulsing, her lungs drowning in her own blood.

Elizabeth instinctively started to help her, but the banker whirled her around as Weed took a step toward the fallen woman, ready to give her a sort of mercy with another bullet, but Ruby O'Banion was past pain now. Weed holstered the .44 and wiped his sweaty hands on the front of his jeans.

Sam took that moment to step out from the side of the building with the wagon tongue upraised in both hands.

"Run, girl!" he yelled, throwing the timber flat at the two men who were for that one instant vulnerable.

Elizabeth ducked and ran to one side.

Sark took the timber across his broad back, giving Weed time to dodge, step back, and go for his six-gun.

Sam saw the maneuver, whirled aside, and started his own draw a half second late.

Weed had always figured he could draw and kill his man in a quarter of a second at close range, but Sam's sudden move made him hurry. His bullet missed Sam's heart by two feet, as it slammed into his right hip before Sam's own .44 came up to fire.

Backing into the open workshop, Weed fired again, but Sam was already knocked down and thrown off to the left.

Sark came running back, his .36 Colt ready to finish off Sam, when Sam fired a desperation shot which, coming on an upward angle, caught Sark's right elbow, coursed up the humerus and out the shoulder at the joint.

Sark screamed in pain, and plunged into the workshop, blocking Weed's kill shot for a second.

Shoving the porky banker aside, Weed aimed again at Sam's upper chest. Smiling, he squeezed the trigger just as Elizabeth came running across from the side, threw her weight against the open door, and slammed it shut.

The bullet was deflected by the plank door, and as Weed pushed against the door with all his strength, Elizabeth snapped the padlock closed.

The single pane of glass gave only enough light for Weed to find it, and knock it out with his six-gun.

"Look out, Sam!" Elizabeth cried as she heard the windowpane break.

Sam turned and fired at the window and heard Weed grunt like a kicked pig, then saw the long barrel of the revolver emerge again, Weed's hatchet face framed behind it, the icy eyes sighting in Sam.

Sam quickly snapped off another round that sent splinters into Weed's face. The bullet ricocheted off cast iron, then Sam heard the sound of breaking glass.

Twice more he fired to drive Weed back from the small single window, and over the acrid odor of burned gunpowder, he smelled the reek of leaking sulfuric acid mixed with the volatile coal oil and alcohol, and he heard Sark lunge against the door, yelling, "Be careful, Weed!"

Then Sam's hammer fell on an empty chamber. As he rolled aside, he saw the hatchet face appear again, the steel barrel steady, the thumb's webbing cocking the single action, the knuckle squeezing and the hammer dropping.

The Colt's bloom of flame caught and fired the rising vapors of refined combustibles, and made a small, crumping explosion as the fire raced instantly back to broken jars of fuming fuel.

Flames roared up through the workshop, and the screams of Sark and Weed became unearthly howls from hell. Their bodies thudded against the locked door, and Elizabeth, unable to stand the ululations of horror and agony, ran to the door. She would have unlocked it for the doomed men, but Sark had taken the key, and in his panic forgot it was his only means of escape.

"The key!" Elizabeth screamed, but both men were beyond hearing.

In mindless panic they slammed their bodies against the plank door again and again as the fire slowly burned their flesh until, still screaming, they fell to the burning floor.

"Come away, girl," Sam groaned. She helped him crawl to safety in the alley.

Clear of the burning shed, Sam saw Skofer tottering toward them, a ghastly smile on his bloody, chalk white features.

"Reporting for duty, Cap'n," he whispered.

"At ease, Sergeant . . ." Sam closed his eyes, and putting his hands over his ears, he tried to forget the screams of the burning.

13

The prairie wind wove its own keening lament over the hill that looked out over the Saline Valley, where the river meandered from the bright mountains toward the Gulf of Mexico far, far away.

The graveyard was so new, there were only two crosses marking recent graves. Already slightly weathered, the cross at the west end of a mound of earth said WILLIAM FARADAY. The newer cross next to it was lettered RUBY O'BANION.

Nothing else.

What was left of Sark's and Weed's remains wasn't recognizable, and no one knew if those were their real names, so they'd been put in a hole together with Armenescu, near the bottom of the hill where they wouldn't bother anything.

Standing by the graves, Sam stood as straight as he could with Elizabeth on his right and Skofer on his left.

Just down the slope waited the surrey, the matched team swishing their tails at horseflies, stamping their hooves occasionally.

On the floor in back were two singed tin boxes covered by a buffalo robe.

"Where will you go from Topeka?" Sam asked Elizabeth.

"I don't know. . . ." She shook her head. "I'm still not right from all the trouble."

"I know what you mean." Sam nodded. "I thought I'd heard the worst in the world, but I can't seem to shake those two loose from my mind."

"You both need to get away and rest up some," Skofer added wisely.

Sam looked into her blue eyes and tried to hold back, but his heart overrode his good sense, and he said, "We could spend some time out West, excepting my cinch is some frayed and I don't travel like a colt no more."

Looking up into his weathered and scarred face, she saw the kindness in him, the lonely homelessness in him, the iron strength and granite in him, and replied, "I'm a spinster already."

"I'd say you're both bad bargains," Skofer said. "Where do I fit in?"

"Gosh, Skofe," Sam said, "I thought you was set on a singing career with old Rip."

"I guess I could do that," Skofer croaked, and dabbed at his eyes with the corner of his bandanna. "Exceptin' old Rip already has a good home."

"Maybe you'd like to go with us," Elizabeth said gently.

"I guess I could do that, too," Skofer said as he perked up, "exceptin' I wouldn't want to be in the way."

184

"You won't be in the way, Skofe." Sam smiled. "You can drive the surrey, and we'll just sit in the back and listen to you sing."

"I don't know. . . ." Skofer muttered. "Maybe I better ask old Rip if he wants to come along."